The Key

K.M. CHANDLER

Printed in the United States of America

First Printing, 2019

ISBN: 978-1-7342094-0-2 (Paperback Edition)
ISBN: 978-1-7342094-1-9 (Ebook Edition)

www.kmchandler.us

To my father
who showed me the power of a story
and sparked my love for the written word

CHAPTER 1

THE STRANGER

"I'll never forget you!" The words echoed through Ember-lynn's head.

As she slowly drifted back into consciousness, her hands fumbled in the dark for the familiar object around her neck. She had spent countless hours running her hands over it, hoping she could remember what it meant if only she tried hard enough. Alas, the cold silver key resting in her hands remained a distant and clouded memory. And yet those words had run through her mind nearly every waking moment, and had even found their way into the secrets of her dreams.

"I'll never forget you..."

"What is so special about this?" she thought as she tucked it safely back inside her nightgown.

She didn't know what part the object played in her past, but it was a part she desperately wanted to remember. It seemed that so many years had passed since the carefree days of her childhood and she began to doubt that she could ever find the memory so deeply buried in the corners of her mind. But, for the moment, she had more important matters to deal with. With this in mind, she took a deep breath to clear her head and reluctantly rolled out of bed. Just then, she heard a soft knock on the door.

"Miss Emberlynn! Princess!" came a voice from outside.

"Come in Margaret, I'm awake," She replied, flatly.

"And it's a good thing, Your Highness," said her maidservant, opening the door and entering the room. "Your father is growing impatient. You know he has plans for you to meet more suitors today and he likes to get an early start."

Emberlynn groaned. "I don't want to meet any more of my father's absurd suitors!" she pouted. "I am seventeen years old and my father is forcing me to choose a complete stranger and marry him. This is so unfair, not to mention ridiculous! I'm not ready to get married!"

"I'm sorry, Princess. I'd change it if I could, but I can't do anything."

"I don't like any of them and I certainly don't love them!" Princess Emberlynn exclaimed.

"Calm down now, Miss, and let me help you get dressed."

Reluctantly Emberlynn crossed the room and allowed Margaret to help her into her dress. It fit perfectly over her slim figure as her long, blonde hair flowed delicately down her back. The deep blue shade of the dress brought out the sapphire color of her piercing eyes.

"Another day in the life of royalty," she sighed.

Emberlynn's father, King Edric, ruled the kingdom of Ardia, which lay between the Banwen Mountains on the West and the Plains of Ginneroth on the East. It was the largest and most influential kingdom in the land. This related in part to the fact that, of all the rulers, King Edric was the most loved by his people. He often walked in the villages that neighbored the castle complex, accompanied by the head of his guard. There he spoke with the citizens, keeping in touch with their views and feelings, and making them feel valued. The princess, however, was rarely allowed to leave the palace grounds. Her father claimed that it was for her safety, and though Emberlynn was sure he meant well, she felt like a bird locked in a very small cage, yearning to fly.

The palace of Ardia was, admittedly, quite grand and beautiful. Perched on a small rise just on the edge of the capital city of Eiladuén, it could be seen for miles. Its white stone towers rose to greet the sun on a cloudless day and the Ardian flag flew high in the morning breeze, proudly displaying the kingdom's crest. The flag was a deep, rich green upon which lay the gold crest—two ivory stallions rearing up toward each other, framed in delicate filigree. They looked free, as if they would gallop away at any moment. Emberlynn wished she could climb upon one and ride away, but this was real life.

She spent much of her time poring over old books in the library or curling up with them in odd corners of the palace where people rarely went. Nothing exciting ever happened at the palace. Yes, there were balls and parties but, after a few dozen, they start to lose their allure. All she really wanted was to experience something new and exciting—but she wasn't holding her breath.

"Sweetie, so nice of you to join us," said King Edric as his daughter sat down at the breakfast table.

"Morning Father, morning Mother," Emberlynn said, forcing a smile on her porcelain face.

"I need you, ready to go, in the throne room by 9:00," her father said sharply. "So hurry up and finish your breakfast."

"Finish!? I haven't even started!" protested Emberlynn.

"Well then you'd better eat quickly, because it's 8:15 already. It isn't my fault you chose to sleep in so late this morning."

Emberlynn forced down a few bites of her breakfast. Although the food at the palace was wonderful, she didn't have much of an appetite. The thought of arrogant, thirty-something-year-old noblemen competing for access to her wealth and title made her stomach turn. It made her feel like a prime piece of property instead of a person who deserved happiness.

"Mother, may I please be excused?" the princess asked, after a few minutes.

"Why Darling, you've barely touched your food!" said the queen.

"I'm not hungry this morning," she replied flatly.

"Alright," said her mother slowly. "But you have less than forty minutes until your father wants you in the throne room."

"All right, Mother," she said through a forced, sweet smile; but as she turned around it transformed into a scowl.

As much as she hated the thought of another day of being accosted by suitors, Emberlynn knew she had no choice; she had to obey her father. So she ascended the stairs as slowly as possible, dragging her feet the entire way.

Once in her room, she closed the door and sank into the comfy chair in front of her mirror. She pulled the key from beneath her dress and let her fingers explore it once more. Emberlynn lost all track of time as she stared at her impassive reflection in the mirror, holding the mysterious trinket that haunted her dreams. As she let her mind wander, visions from her past crept slowly into her mind. They were independent images and disconnected thoughts; a garden full of roses, a pale pink dress, the moon, the stars, the sea... They flashed through her mind one at a time. She didn't know when or where, but she knew she'd seen all of them before. They were pieces of separate and unspecific memories. She was comforted by these images.

They seemed safe and familiar, even if she couldn't name the time or place. It must have been long ago and so far from here...

The next thing she knew, her mother was banging on her bedroom door.

"Emberlynn, dear!" she called. "You are ten minutes late and the first suitor is already here! Your father will be furious if you keep him waiting any longer, so you had better hurry!"

Emberlynn pulled herself back to reality. She tucked the key safely away under her dress and took a moment to calm herself before pasting that fake smile on her face that she'd become so accustomed to. Then she opened the door.

"Sorry, Mother. I just wanted to make sure I looked my absolute best for the suitors," she lied.

Her mother gave her a look that showed she didn't believe her but wasn't going to push the matter. They walked briskly to the throne room and Emberlynn entered gracefully.

"Sorry to keep you waiting, Father," she said lightly as she crossed the room and ascended the steps to her throne.

"I...I couldn't decide how I wanted to wear my hair today," she said slowly.

It was a lame excuse, she knew, but it was the first thing she thought of and her father and suitor both seemed to accept it. No harm done.

"Ah, Sire!" exclaimed the suitor, a slender man with black hair and a narrow mustache.

"Your daughter is even more beautiful than I imagined!"

He bowed to Emberlynn, took her petite hand, and kissed it. "Allow me to introduce myself," he said, standing up straight.

"I am Sir Reginald, Lord of Idiers."

With these words the pompous air that surrounded him seemed to grow.

"How lovely," she thought. *"Another rich, arrogant fool. More like Reginald, Lord of the Idiots,"* she mused. *"Such a pity, too; he's not half bad looking."*

For the next two hours Emberlynn pretended to listen with interest to all Reginald said. She didn't catch more than a few words, though, as she was too busy trying not to be sick at the thought of spending an entire afternoon with a whole series of Reginalds. They were all the same, these suitors. She had never met a single one she could even tolerate. Her father didn't seem to understand that, because he kept bringing her more of the same. And this, she knew, was her destiny: to refuse suitor after suitor, until her father either gave up—unlikely—or grew tired of her obstinance and forced her to marry a man she could never care for.

"Well it was lovely to see you again, Reggie," Emberlynn heard her father say, finally. This pulled her back to the present. "I do hope you will be attending our ball in a few months."

"Of course, Sire!" was the enthusiastic reply. With that, Reginald bowed to Emberlynn again and exited the room.

"Ball?" questioned Emberlynn, after a moment's pause.

"Yes," her father replied.

"What ball?"

"The one your mother and I are throwing in two months, to celebrate your eighteenth birthday," he said, unable to suppress a smile.

"Oh no!" she protested; she knew that look.

"You mean to tell me you and Mother are throwing a ball and inviting all the eligible males in the kingdom, because you want me to choose a suitor to marry?!" she asked angrily, already knowing the answer.

"Of course not..." he said, matter-of-factly. "We're only inviting the ones with titles."

She was speechless in disbelief.

"Look Emberlynn, I know you aren't thrilled with the idea, but you're almost eighteen and it's time you found a husband," he stated, firmly.

Then he sighed.

"You know, I'm not trying to be mean; I'm doing this because I care about you. I want what's best for you and although I know you don't like the way it appears, it's best that you finally settle on a suitor."

"Father, has it ever crossed your mind that I don't like any of your suitors?! And they certainly don't like me!" she retorted.

"They're only after my money and title, and they're all much too old for me anyway! I know you love me, but don't you think I should have some say in my life?" She paused for a moment before adding, "The least you could do is find a suitor I might actually like for a change, but it seems there's not a single man like that in our entire kingdom! Not in all of Ardia."

She let out a deep sigh.

Then something completely unexpected happened: the king smiled.

"What...?" his daughter asked slowly, surprised.

"I see," he said, with a mysterious grin toying at the corners of his mouth. "Well, if that's how you feel..."

If the king's reaction had shocked Emberlynn, it was nothing compared to what happened next.

The king turned around and, without another word, walked to the door of the throne room and opened it.

Emberlynn sat on her throne with a puzzled look on her face. Then her father stepped aside, and she saw him. She had never seen anyone quite like him before. He was a head taller than her father, with blonde hair that was cut short, and ice blue eyes.

"He can't be more than twenty," she thought, in disbelief.

"Is he a squire bringing a message to my father?"

She was able to tear her eyes away from his handsome face long enough to notice his clothes. He was dressed far too elegantly to be a squire.

"Okay, that rules out that possibility. No...he couldn't possibly be....he doesn't look anything at all like a suitor. But..."

Then she noticed the ring on his finger. The crest was one of Lemethian nobility. She let out a gasp, too quiet for anyone but herself to hear. Had her father finally brought her a decent suitor? She glanced over at the king, and the smile on his face gave the welcome answer.

The young man entered the room and walked, ever so slowly, toward her. Then he did something no other suitor had ever done before: he looked her straight in the eye. He didn't give her an appraising look, as the others had. He didn't immediately speak and try to flatter her. He just stood there at the base of the steps and stared into her eyes. Emberlynn held his gaze. Then a soft, sweet smile formed slowly on his lips. There was something about his smile that made her feel as though she had known him her entire life. The strangest feeling stirred in the pit of her stomach.

Her father hurried over to them. "Allow me to introduce my daughter, Emberlynn, Princess of Ardia."

The young suitor bowed slightly but remained silent.

"Emberlynn, this is Banning," her father said softly. "He is the son of Theron, Duke of Kingston."

"Kingston?" Emberlynn asked her father quietly, finally finding the courage to speak. "Isn't that in Uncle Thomas' kingdom?"

"Yes, Dear," he replied. "It's in the kingdom of Lemeth."

So she had been right about the ring. Lemeth was the kingdom just south of Ardia, bordering the Tavys River. King

Thomas was brother to Queen Gwyneria, who had married Edric when he became King, and moved to Ardia. Emberlynn and her parents visited occasionally, and these trips were the only time she was allowed to leave the palace. Though it had been many years since she was last there, she loved Lemeth, and was always eager hear stories of places outside the palace walls.

"This suitor could be exactly the excitement I'm looking for," the princess thought.

She turned to him and smiled—not a fake, imitation smile like she usually did, but a genuine one. She couldn't remember the last time she'd truly smiled; the kind that lights up your entire face and radiates in your eyes, but that is what she did now.

Then she stood and curtsied before saying, "It's a pleasure to meet you, Banning."

"You as well, Your Highness," he replied.

His voice was gentle and smooth. He radiated charm and her heart began to beat a little faster.

"Please," she replied, a little surprised, "Call me Emberlynn."

"Emberlynn..." he said slowly, smiling again.

After a moment's silence gazing into those hypnotizing ice blue eyes, Emberlynn managed to speak again.

"So tell me, what's it like living in Lemeth? I've been a few times to visit my uncle and his family, but it's been so long I hardly remember a thing about it."

"It's beautiful there. We live only five miles from the castle, at Whitehawk Estate, at the base of the most picturesque mountains you've ever seen. They're topped with snow all year round."

He was speaking only when spoken to; answering her questions fully yet succinctly. There was something incredibly refreshing about that after listening to countless suitors brag about themselves for hours on end. Banning seemed different—reserved, almost shy. Or perhaps he was just respectful. Either way, she found him intriguing.

"How lovely!" she exclaimed. "Tell me more..."

"Well," he continued. "The people there are wonderful—always so friendly. Your uncle, King Thomas, is a close friend of my father, so we spend lots of time at the palace."

"And what is the palace like?"

Banning hesitated for a moment, obviously thinking carefully about his next words.

"Enchanting..." he replied, finally. "As, forgive my bluntness...," he added quietly, "...are you."

This was so very much unlike the flattery she was constantly bombarded with. It seemed...sincere. Emberlynn's heart melted at these words.

She blushed furiously but smiled and said, "And you as well."

The king took advantage of the silence that followed and asked Banning if he would like to join them for an early lunch.

"I'd love to. Thank you, Sir," was his reply.

"Emberlynn..." he said, holding out an arm for her.

She beamed and took it, and Banning escorted her out of the throne room and into the dining hall.

"Please cancel all other suitor appointments for today," the king instructed his counselor quietly as they passed on the way out of the throne room.

Emberlynn picked at her food through the entire meal, much more interested in what Banning was saying. He told her about growing up in Lemeth and recounted several of the adventures he and his father had been part of. She sat there wistfully, wishing she could relate to these tales of daring and excitement; most of her life had been lived inside the palace walls.

Emberlynn, unwilling to part with Banning so soon, suggested they take him on a tour of the palace—a plan with which the king and Banning both readily agreed. They spent the afternoon traipsing around the castle and its grounds as the princess and her father showed Banning all her favorite places. Before she knew it, they were being called for the evening meal and it was time for Banning to leave.

"I do hope to see more of you before you return home," said Emberlynn.

"Of course! I'm staying just a short distance from here, in the charming estate of Westin Abbey. And I won't be leaving until after the ball, which His Majesty was so kind to mention during lunch."

"How delightful!" replied the princess.

"Perhaps you'd like to join me for an afternoon ride tomorrow?" he questioned. "I hear Ardia has the finest horses of all the great kingdoms."

"Well I certainly think so. I'm quite partial to my own mare—a purebred Arabian and black as night."

"I'd love to see her. Does this mean I can count on you tomorrow?"

"I suppose," she replied, coyly, hiding her enthusiasm.

"I look forward to it. Shall I meet you at the castle gate around 2 o'clock?"

"I'll be there."

CHAPTER 2

THE DUKE OF KINGSTON

That night Emberlynn's dreams didn't feature the key as they almost always had before. She was haunted by a new dream—dark, cold, and mysterious. She couldn't make sense of most of it, seeing shadowy figures through a dense fog. She heard a voice calling her name. Its owner took her hand and tried to pull her away from the approaching figures. "Run!" they yelled, their voice metallic, as if it was coming from the other end of a long tunnel. She tried to flee but couldn't move; it was as if her feet were made of lead, cemented to the ground. Her hand was released and whoever had held it disappeared into the haze as the other figures became clearer. She continued to struggle with her feet, but it was useless. The figures finally reached her. Through the fog she could barely make out a triumphant smile; cold as ice and eerily sinister. It was the kind of smile that said, "All my plans are falling into place."

She woke with a start and sat up in bed. She could still feel the horror of her dream, see the icy smile. Terror was pulsing through her veins. Something about this dream seemed vaguely familiar, like a piece of a puzzle she was desperately trying to assemble.

"Snap out of it, Ember!" she instructed herself. "It was only a dream. It was only a dream. It was only a dream..." she repeated.

The princess walked around the palace in a haze all morning, tired and preoccupied from her fitful night. Nevertheless, that afternoon, she kept her promise and was waiting for Banning at 2 o'clock with her mare, Artemis. They took a leisurely ride around the palace grounds, laughing together all the while. Emberlynn felt completely at ease in Banning's company, and all thoughts of her frightful dream were soon driven from her mind. After their ride they took tea in the garden, enjoying their time together as the shadows grew long. When Emberlynn said goodbye to Banning, she returned to the palace with a smile on her face and a flush in her cheeks.

From that day, Emberlynn and Banning were inseparable. It wasn't long before everyone at court noticed a change in the princess; the girl who had once been politely disinterested in palace affairs, and often listless, was now full of life. In the rare moments she was seen without Banning, she could be found strolling through the gardens or halls of the palace, singing merrily to herself.

Banning impressed Emberlynn with his ease with horses (something the people of Ardia valued greatly) and his knowledge of the world outside the Ardian borders (which the princess prized above all). He had a knack for making stories come alive, and Emberlynn almost imagined she was with him as he trekked through the Banwen Mountains and sailed across the Denberlaé Sea. They spent nearly every day together and Banning's hold on the princess grew with every meeting. Everyone could tell she was smitten. But these days were a double-edged sword.

In the weeks that followed, Emberlynn was visited by her nightmare more than once. It varied a little from time to time—sometimes she was able to move a few steps, other times the figure holding her hand didn't leave her side. But one thing remained constant: it always ended with that sinister smile.

After a few weeks, Banning asked his father to come and meet Emberlynn. His father traveled from Lemeth to Ardia a few days later to see the young lady everyone was talking about and who now commanded most of his son's attention.

"Father!" Banning called as the Duke climbed out of his carriage. "I've missed you! How was your journey?"

"Uneventful. I'm glad to see you, too; it has been far too quiet at home," was the reply.

Emberlynn saw pain the Duke's face and remembered that Banning's mother had died when he was very young. It must have been hard to raise his son alone and even harder to be in a big, empty house when Banning was away. She was sure that he missed his son greatly.

Emberlynn zoomed out from the expression to get a look at the face itself. It was uncanny how much Banning resembled his father. They had the same short, blonde hair, tall muscular figures, and identical charming smiles. And she saw now the source of Banning's unusual ice blue eyes.

"How odd..." thought Emberlynn. *"I've never seen eyes that color."*

Staring into them was like looking out over a glacial lake on a clear, sunny, morning.

"Father, this is Princess Emberlynn," he announced proudly, as he put his hand softly on her shoulder.

"I'm delighted to finally meet you!" the Duke said, enthusiastically.

"Banning has told me so much about you in his letters; he hardly speaks of anything else. My son seems to be quite taken with you. After all, he's been gone more than a month and I understand he plans to stay a month more."

Emberlynn blushed. "We've been having a lot of fun."

"Yes, Father! Emberlynn has been showing me around Eiladuén!" he said excitedly. "It's gorgeous here! Tomorrow she has promised to take me to the fields where they breed the horses."

"Wise choice, young lady..." the Duke jested. "Banning's horse has seen a few too many winters and he could use another one."

"Father, you exaggerate!" Banning laughed.

Indeed laughter filled the rest of the afternoon, as father and son enjoyed their reunion. Emberlynn found the Duke delightful and loved seeing his interactions with the man who had captured her affections. They seemed to get along naturally and effortlessly. In all honesty, she was a little jealous of Banning's relationship with his father. If only her own father were like that: lighthearted and charming. No, the king was strict and hardly ever showed emotion. And they didn't usually get along particularly well.

The sun set much too soon, as it always seemed to do when she was with Banning. He and his father departed to the estate where Banning was staying and Emberlynn struggled up the stairs to her bedroom. She hadn't realized how tired she was until her companions left. She quickly got ready for bed then crawled under the covers for another night of troubled dreams.

At the estate, Banning and his father were discussing the day's activities. The king had been extremely pleased to meet Banning's father. He was grateful that the Duke's son had had changed his daughter's outlook on men. She seemed to now be open to the prospect of accepting a suitor. Edric had personally given him a tour of the castle and the two men got along quite well. Banning had seen the castle interior on numerous occasions, but he and Emberlynn tagged along for the pleasure of the Duke's company. Afterward they had gone on a short ride around the castle grounds, as was their habit.

"You've really got her under your spell," said the Duke, delighted.

"It would seem so. Emberlynn is a remarkable young woman—beautiful, witty, and, yes, totally smitten with me."

"Excellent! She is quite a catch. I think you two will be very happy together. And you will make a fabulous king of Ardia." The Duke's face lit up as he said this. He and Banning had never expected to get this lucky.

∽

"How fascinating!" Emberlynn exclaimed, as Banning finished a riveting tale of one of his many adventures. It was a bright morning in early May, just two days before the ball, and the pair was taking a walk around the castle gardens. "I've never done anything exciting," she admitted, her tone suddenly wistful. "I've spent nearly my entire life inside this castle."

"But you are lucky, Emberlynn," he assured her. "You've been given the gift of royalty. You've got people waiting on you hand and foot. Anything you could ever want is at your fingertips." With these words he reached over and delicately took her hand in his.

The princess felt a chill run down her spine. She stopped walking and looked at him curiously, but did not pull away. "The truth is," she confessed as they resumed walking, hand in hand, "what I really want is to go on an adventure, to feel the excitement of the unknown. Imagine living your whole life never being permitted to take a single risk; being locked away like a fragile porcelain doll, because the whole world's afraid you'll break."

"Ah, but you are a porcelain doll," he replied. "Delicate, flawless, and beautiful. Your father is just protecting you, you know."

"I know, but I don't need quite that much protection. I just wish I could do something exciting."

"Well there are different types of excitement," Banning said mysteriously, a huge grin on his face.

"Oh really? And what might those be?" she inquired playfully.

"You'll just have to wait and see…" he said.

"I have a much better idea," she insisted. "Why don't you tell me right now?"

He shook his head, and the look on his face told her there was no point in pressing the matter.

"You know…" Emberlynn said, teasingly, "Sometimes I think you're almost as stubborn as I am."

"Almost…" he conceded.

They both laughed. They finished their walk and Banning escorted the princess back to the castle door.

"I have some important things to attend to tomorrow, but I shall see you the day after, at the ball," he said in parting.

Emberlynn gave him a wondering look but knew she wasn't going to get anymore information out of him today. She would just have to wait. So she smiled and nodded her assent.

Banning began to walk away, but stopped suddenly and looked over his shoulder. "Would you do me honor of saving the first dance for me?" he called.

"I would be delighted," she called back.

Banning turned again and walked down the lane to his carriage, a skip in his step. Emberlynn watched him drive away and disappear down the long castle drive. Then she hurried inside, her heart racing. She couldn't wait for the ball.

Chapter 3

DEJA VU

The next two days were a blur. The entire palace was in a frenzy as servants and cooks prepared for the upcoming ball. The scent of roasted meats wafted through the halls, accompanied by the delicate aroma of apple pastries—a favorite of the princess. Rich tapestries of ivory and green, bearing the royal crest of Ardia and accented with an array of ornamental colors, were hung throughout the palace. The king and queen spared no expense to demonstrate to their distinguished guests the strength and riches of their kingdom, and to Banning and his father the value of a most intimate alliance with Ardia.

Emberlynn emerged only at meal times, and once more for the final fitting of her gown. The remainder of the time she spent tucked away in her room to avoid the stress and havoc that was found almost everywhere else in the castle. And she thought of Banning.

The evening of Emberlynn's eighteenth birthday finally arrived and brought with it the greatest ball the kingdom had ever seen. It was the most anticipated event in recent memory—perhaps since the king and queen's own wedding, more than two decades earlier. Every eligible bachelor of high

18

birth from the surrounding kingdoms was invited, along with carefully chosen companions. The high born and influential of Ardia all hoped they would receive invitations as well; it was a rare opportunity to mix and gain favor with the rulers, as well as to be seen by others in position.

The guests were set to begin arriving at eight o'clock. The clock struck six and Emberlynn's gown was delivered to her room by four maidservants who helped her into it and spent the next two hours getting her ready. They set her golden hair in curls and pinned them atop her head, leaving a few strands falling gently on either side of her face. Her dress was a deep shade of green which, together her pale ivory skin, paid homage to the royal colors of the kingdom of Ardia. It cinched in at the waist, showing off her petite figure, then fanned outward, reaching all the way to the floor. There were diamonds stitched into the bodice, as well as throughout the long train, and large teardrop emeralds, set in gold and accented with diamonds, hung sparkling from her ears. And the finishing touch: a pale pink color was smoothed over her cheeks and lips, which shimmered softly as they caught the light.

By the time they were finished, Emberlynn looked more like a goddess than the young woman who, not so long ago, sported messy hair and played hide-and-seek among the castle's many rooms. She had always been a pretty girl, but there was something about that dark green dress and the way her soft golden locks framed her delicate face that made her radiate beauty. She felt like someone out of a history book—Cinderella, Snow White, or Sleeping Beauty... the legendary queens of old. Their magic seemed to have died with them; nothing like their stories had happened in hundreds of years, but the idea was still inspiring. However they managed it, they had all made their mark on history as some of the most beloved rulers the world had ever seen. And their stories all ended the same way: *"And they lived happily ever after..."* Maybe this would be the night she would find her own Happily Ever After. She knew that after tonight nothing would ever be the same. It was the beginning of her story, and she couldn't wait to see where it would take her.

The clock struck eight and the guests began to arrive. The queen knocked softly on her daughter's door.

"Come in!" called Emberlynn.

"I brought you something," said her mother. She held out the most beautiful necklace Emberlynn had ever seen.

"Oh Mother!" she said, nearly breathless at its beauty.

"I want you to have this. It was given to me on my eighteenth birthday."

"Mother, your necklace?! I don't know what to say! Thank you! I know how much it means to you."

"It was made by the fairies, you know..." Queen Gwyneria recited, as she fastened the necklace around her daughter's neck.

"When your great grandfather was younger, he saved the life of a fairy princess. If you save a fairy's life, they give you a vial of fairy dust in return. Your great grandfather had the fairies compress that vial into gemstones and craft them into a necklace as a wedding present for my grandmother."

Emberlynn sneezed, suddenly. She scrunched up her nose, scratched it gently and said,

"Sorry, mother. Keep going..."

"Are you alright, Sweetie?"

"Yes, I am," she replied. "I've felt a bit worn down lately, but I expect it's just the stress of planning for the ball."

"Well, that bit's over now," said the queen. "All that's left for you to do is attend the ball. And that's the fun bit."

Emberlynn smiled.

"And maybe tonight I'll get a proper night's rest," she said. "But you were in the middle of the story of the necklace. Don't stop on my account."

Queen Gwyneria continued.

"My grandmother gave the necklace to my mother on the day of her wedding, and my mother gave it to me on my eighteenth birthday. I'm sure she would have passed it on at my wedding, but since I didn't marry your father until I was nineteen..." She laughed. "And now, I want you to have it."

Emberlynn was speechless as she embraced her mother in a tender hug.

"Yes, well..." said the queen. "We mustn't keep our guests waiting. Are you ready?"

Emberlynn nodded. Her mother exited the room and waited for her in the hallway. Once she was sure she was alone, she carefully and hesitantly removed the key from around her neck, tucking it safely beneath her pillow. *"I don't know what this is,"* she thought, *"But tonight, it doesn't really matter. All that matters right now is Banning."* It was the first time she had ever taken it off, and it almost felt like a part of her was missing. But she shook off the feeling and took a deep breath. Exhaling, she exited her bedroom, closed the door, and followed her mother to the ball and her waiting guests.

The two made their way to the ballroom, which absolutely sparkled with lights and decorations. The queen entered first, announced by the head of the royal guard. She made her way gracefully down the stairs, through the crowd, and over to the platform on which three thrones stood. There, she took her seat beside her husband.

As soon as she was seated, the door at the top of the stairs opened once more. A hush fell over the room as all heads turned to see the princess.

"Introducing Her Royal Highness Emberlynn, Princess of Ardia!" The guard called across the ballroom.

She seemed to radiate light as she slowly descended the marble staircase. It was as if the world was moving in slow motion; everyone stood in awe. As she reached the bottom of the stairs, the crowd parted and the princess made her way to the throne on the other side of her father. Then the king stood and addressed his guests.

"Thank you all for joining us for this momentous occasion; we are honored by your presence here. Tonight we celebrate the eighteenth birthday of our beautiful and beloved daughter, Emberlynn!" As you know, this marks her legal ascendance to adulthood and makes official her qualification to succeed me one day as monarch of the Kingdom of Ardia. At that time I have no doubt that she will distinguish herself in service to the land and people she so dearly loves. Honored guests, I give you Emberlynn, Crown Princess of Ardia!"

At that, the chief of the royal guard prompted, "Hail Emberlynn! Crown Princess of Ardia," which the crowd enthusiastically echoed —"Hail Emberlynn!" The princess blushed at this show of affection and bowed her head slightly in acknowledgement of the crowd, her eyes misting with appreciation.

King Edric concluded with, "We hope you will enjoy a wonderful time with us here this evening. And now let the dancing begin!" At that the orchestra stuck a favorite tune of the people, who began stirring to take partners for the dance.

Emberlynn scanned the crowd for any sign of Banning, but found none. Her face fell. A handsome stranger approached her. "May I have this dance, Your Highness?" She paused, considering, until she saw a tall man with short blonde hair making his way across the room, toward her. She smiled apologetically.

"I'm sorry, but I already promised the first dance to someone else."

"I understand," he replied. "Perhaps the next one?"

"Perhaps," she responded politely.

Banning quickly ascended the steps to the dais and took her hands. "I'm sorry to keep you waiting, Emberlynn," he apologized, "but I have a surprise for you that wasn't quite ready."

She looked at him quizzically.

"And don't bother asking, because I'm not going to tell you what it is yet!" he scolded.

"All right, all right," she conceded.

"Shall we?" he asked, extending his hand and inclining his head in the direction of the dance floor.

"We shall indeed" the princess responded.

The pair made their way to the middle of the dance floor. After a short bow and a deep breath, Banning took her in his arms and they began to move with the music.

"Emberlynn, I must say, you look absolutely breathtaking this evening!"

"Thank you, Banning," she said, blushing.

The musicians were playing upbeat songs and gentlemen were spinning ladies across the floor. The room was a blur of brilliant color and constant motion. After four or five of these tunes, they began playing a slower waltz. It took her a moment to realize what was happening, but before she knew it Banning had pulled her close and they were striking graceful circles in the center of the room. Emberlynn felt a strange exhilaration being in Banning's arms.

At the song's conclusion Banning grabbed Emberlynn's hand and guided her firmly across the ballroom, away from the crowd. As he did so, a strange smile crossed his face. It was unlike the sweet smile she had become accustomed to, that always made her heart beat faster. It was cold, like ice, matching his eyes.

"Banning, you're hurting me!" she cried.

He loosened his grip on her wrist. "I'm sorry..." he said, apologetically. "I'm just so excited!" he added, the smile returning. There was something about that smile that made her feel uneasy, almost frightened. He continued dragging her through the crowd—less forcefully, but with equal determination.

"What are you doing?" she asked, when they were finally free and making their way across the balcony.

When they reached the bench in the middle, he pushed her onto it and took a seat beside her. He hesitated for a moment, then took a deep breath and said, "Asking you to marry me." He retrieved a small velvet box from his jacket pocket and opened it, revealing a gorgeous gold ring. It featured an enormous diamond surrounded by smaller stones that accented its radiance.

"I....I..." she stammered, shocked and at a complete loss for words. "I...don't know what to say."

His smile grew. No, not quite a smile.... more of a smirk—a cold, almost evil, overconfident smirk. It was the kind of look that said, "All my plans are falling into place."

She knew that look; since she'd met Banning it had haunted her dreams almost as often as the key. But while the key brought peace and warmth, this look shot fear through her entire body. She knew that look...she knew that look...why did she know that look? She was suddenly overwhelmed with the feeling that she never should have taken off the key. Terror pulsed through her veins. She didn't know why, but she felt somehow vulnerable without it. At that moment, she would have traded anything to have it around her neck. But that was not an option. *For the love of... snap out of it, Ember!* she thought. *"You have to stay focused!"*

"Say you will, please say you will!" Banning said.

"This is just so...unexpected," she managed, her hands beginning to shake.

The smirk began to fade and he gave her a strange look.

"Are you cold?" Banning asked, flatly.

"N-n-no..." she stammered. "Just....surprised."

She could tell he was getting angry and she realized then that he mustn't sense any change in her. She mustered all her courage and heard herself say, "I do care about you, I just feel like we're both so young."

"Emberlynn," he said reassuringly, the ice cold smile returning, "Both our parents were about our age when they were married. Most royals marry at this age, or younger."

"I know, but there's so much I want to do with my life," she argued. He looked her in the eyes and she wanted to run away. She wanted to run as far and as fast as her legs would carry her, but she couldn't move. She could hardly breathe. Then she said, "I just need a little time to...uh...get used to the idea."

Her head started swimming and her mind was slowly becoming cloudy. She suddenly felt lightheaded and cold. After a few seconds, though it seemed like an eternity, she tore her eyes away from Banning's. As she did so, her mind began to clear.

Just then she looked up and saw her father coming toward them.

"Oh great," she thought. *"Just what I need."*

"So," the king began. "Do we have a wedding to plan?" He was beaming.

"Uh...um..." stammered Emberlynn.

The king heard the hesitation in his daughter's voice and turned to Banning.

"She 'needs a little time to get used to the idea,'" said Banning, disappointment obvious on his face and in his voice.

"Ah...naturally she's a little nervous." The king assured him, sensing his confusion and resentment at Emberlynn's hesitation. "She's always like this when it comes to big things. Why, she didn't even want to have this ball at first! Of course once she warmed up to the idea she's been absolutely overwhelmed with excitement."

This seemed to satisfy Banning and he smiled once more. It was almost back to normal, but there was still a trace of mischief in it, and it made Emberlynn sick to her stomach. *"I thought I loved him,"* she told herself. *"Why should a smile mean anything? Why should it ruin my perfect romance?"* She looked up at him and it sent shivers down her spine again. She no longer felt anything for him. However unexplainable and strange it was, one smile was all it took to cure her of her infatuation.

"Won't you excuse us for a moment?" The king asked Banning. "Just a little father-daughter chat."

Banning nodded and disappeared into the crowd. The king took Emberlynn's arm and pulled her to the far edge of the balcony. "What is going on, young lady?!" he demanded. "I thought you loved Banning. Why are you hesitating?"

"I...I don't know," she replied, sheepishly.

She knew she couldn't tell him the truth. *"Oh, you know... there was something in his smile that filled me with fear and suddenly I find him utterly repulsive. And this is all because it seems familiar; because I saw that smile in a dream, well, nightmare..."* she thought, sarcastically. *"Yeah...that'll go over really well."* But she knew she had to think of something. She couldn't marry him...she just couldn't!

"I just needed a moment to think. It's a bit sudden."

"He's been courting you for two months, Emberlynn!"

"Yes, well. I just don't know if I'm ready for marriage."

"You complained that I never brought you a suitor you liked and that no one in the kingdom was good enough. So, I bring you a wonderful, handsome, young man from Lemeth who is a personal friend of your uncle and you are totally smitten with!! And you won't marry him?!"

The king's face was turning red. He had lost his patience. It was just as Emberlynn feared, he was going to force her to marry. She knew there was no way out. Or was there...? Suddenly an idea occurred to her. She knew it wasn't going to be easy, but she also knew in her heart it was the only way.

"Well I have news for you, young lady! You're going to go back in there right now and tell Banning you're going to marry him!"

"Of course I'm going to marry him!" she said quickly. "I just needed some time to make sure it was what I really wanted to do. And I've decided it is."

The king's face was a mix of shock and relief. He let out a deep sigh. "Good."

She mustered her sweetest smile and followed her father back to the ball. Banning greeted her at the door, a hopeful smile on his face. It was the one he'd worn the day they met. Her heart threatened to melt again, but her head wouldn't let it. *"No!"* she told herself. *"One sweet smile doesn't make up for what I felt."* She had seen his dark side, even if no one else had. *"He should have been more understanding of my hesitation. He didn't know the reason for it. He had no right to be angry and harsh."*

"I'm sorry for my hesitation. I wanted to make sure it was the right decision. And I've decided it is," she told him.

Banning was thrilled. He pulled her close and kissed her sweetly on the cheek. "I'm so glad!" he said, letting out a sigh of relief. "I love you so much."

She knew she should have responded in kind so he didn't get suspicious, but she couldn't make the words come out. She squeezed his hand and smiled. She and Banning danced together the rest of the night, the porcelain smile once again pasted on her face. She had to get through this night; her smile had to stay.

Finally, after what Emberlynn was sure was the longest night of her life, the guests began to leave. Banning was telling her all about his plans for their future, but she didn't hear a word.

"What do you think? Emberlynn? Emberlynn!?" Banning's voice broke through her trance.

"Oh, I'm sorry. I'm just so tired. What was the question?"

"I want to go home and tell my friends and servants about our engagement before we announce it officially."

"Of course. But...hurry back, won't you, Dear?" she managed. The words burned her mouth, but she had to make him believe she wanted this.

"I hope you'll excuse me, but I really must be getting to bed. There's been so much excitement today, I'm positively exhausted."

"Until we meet again..." he said, pressing her hand softly to his lips.

With that, they parted—Banning back to Lemeth to begin preparations for the wedding, and Emberlynn to her room to make her own preparations. She would leave tonight, before anyone realized what was happening. She couldn't marry Banning. She didn't understand why or how, but she knew he wasn't the charming gentleman she had originally thought. There was something much too familiar—and sinister—about him that she hadn't noticed before; something that scared her. She couldn't put her finger on it or explain why she should react so strongly to a mere dream. But she knew, with more certainty than she had ever known anything before, that she had to go away. She hoped she had done an adequate job at convincing her father she truly wanted to marry Banning. If she had, they wouldn't know the reason for her sudden disappearance. They would search for her, and she would make sure she was impossible to find. But just in case, she was going to hurry. She didn't have a moment to lose.

CHAPTER 4

FIGHT OR FLIGHT

The first thing Emberlynn did when she reached her room was lock the door. Her mind was racing and she was having trouble thinking straight. She walked directly to her bed, pulled the key from under her pillow, and replaced the fairy necklace with the plain and familiar trinket. The princess felt calmer and more secure with it around her neck, and allowed herself a moment to breathe and collect her thoughts; if she was going to pull this off, she needed to have her wits about her.

Emberlynn knew she had to make her escape as soon as possible, so she pulled out a medium sized drawstring bag from her closet and began packing the things she would need for her journey. It was only then that she realized she didn't have any of them; the princess didn't own any clothes that wouldn't immediately give her away as royalty, nor did she have food or supplies for long journey.

"That can be remedied easily enough," she thought, stashing her bag underneath her bed.

"Margaret!" she called to her maidservant.

A few moments later Margaret was at the door of Emberlynn's room.

30

"Yes, Miss?"

"I'd like you to draw my bath, please."

"Right away, Miss!"

Margaret hurried off to heat the water for the princess' bath.

"It usually takes her about twenty minutes..." Emberlynn thought. *"So I'll have plenty of time..."*

She slipped out of her room, tiptoed down the hall, and quietly opened the door to Margaret's quarters; they were near to Emberlynn's in case the princess needed anything. She opened Margaret's drawers and pulled out one patched, bluish-grey dress, a pair of brown pants, and an old off-white peasant style blouse.

"Good, I can easily pass for a higher level peasant in these," she smiled.

It was fortunate that Margaret was about her size, though with a somewhat less-sculpted figure. The clothes would fit reasonably well and their plain fashion would not draw any unwanted attention.

Emberlynn closed the drawer and slipped out of the room, leaving no trace of entrance behind her. She had just enough time to hurry to her room and stash the clothes hurriedly in her bag before Margaret came in and announced that her bath was ready.

"Do you require anything else?" she asked.

"Actually..." said Emberlynn, suddenly realizing she would need food for the journey. "I'm a bit chilly. Could you go and fetch me a few extra blankets for my bed?"

"Of course, Your Highness."

The closet that housed the blankets was on the opposite end of the castle, which would give Emberlynn plenty of time to steal down to the kitchen and take some food. The cooks had the night off after a long day of preparing food for the ball, so the kitchen would be empty. When she reached it, Emberlynn opened the pantry and stashed a few loaves of bread under her robes. Then she grabbed a canteen and filled it with water from the pitcher on the counter.

She turned to exit the kitchen and ran straight into the head cook.

"Princess, what on earth are you doing in the kitchen at this hour?"

"I...uh...wanted a drink of water..." she said, unconvincingly.

"Could Margaret not have gotten it for you?"

"I sent her to fetch me some blankets and I didn't feel like waiting for her to return."

"Of course, Your Highness," he replied. "Can I get you anything else while you're here?"

"No thank you. Don't you have the night off?"

"Ah yes, Your Highness, but I was checking to make sure it was clean before I left for the night. With all the people bustling about this evening, I wanted to make sure things were in good shape for tomorrow's breakfast."

"Well, it's spotless," she said, as she hurried out of the kitchen.

"Goodnight, Your Highness."

"Goodnight."

She practically sprinted back to her room.

That was way too close for comfort! she thought, as she placed the food into her bag alongside Margaret's clothes. *It's a good thing he didn't arrive a moment sooner.*

"Here you are, Miss," said Margaret, who had returned with the blankets. She handed them to Emberlynn. "If you won't be needing anything else, I'll be going to bed now."

"Yes, goodnight Margaret."

"Night, Princess."

With that, Emberlynn was alone. Her immediate thought was to change clothes, drain the bath, and make her escape. Until she looked in the mirror.

"Oh no!" she said aloud, to herself. "I'm still made up for the ball! There's no way I can walk around with my hair up in ringlets!"

The truth was she couldn't walk around with her hair the way it was, regardless. No one else in the entire kingdom had hair like hers; it fell just below her waist, and was a distinct shade of fine, silky blonde. Her hair was her most identifiable feature.

"This isn't good," she said.

She would have to take a bath to wash the style out of her hair, that much was clear. But she realized in that moment that she would have to cut it as well. The thought nauseated her, but she had no choice. If she was going to do this, she'd have to commit to doing it right, whatever it took, and put her whole heart into it.

The princess slipped out of her ball gown and into the bath. As she sat there, washing her hair, she tried to figure out the best way to slip out of the palace unseen. She did know of one secret passage, but the other end of it would no doubt be heavily guarded, especially on the night of such a large-scale event. She couldn't just walk out of the castle.

"Well this does present a problem..." she realized.

About twenty minutes later, when her hair was once again clean and straight and she was climbing out of the tub, she found the answer.

"I have to wait until morning," she admitted to herself, a little disappointed.

If she disappeared from her bed in the middle of the night, it would be painfully obvious that she had run away. She knew she couldn't walk away from the castle in broad daylight, but there was one approach that just might work. Emberlynn dried off, drained the bath, slipped into her nightgown, and climbed unwillingly into bed. The princess knew she wasn't going to get any sleep...she was in for a long night.

Emberlynn sat up with a start. It was the middle of the night and she had been running her plan over and over again in her mind.

"Money!" she cried. "I can't possibly leave the castle without any way to pay for things. Of course I don't have any of that. My father buys me everything. But..."

She remembered that the king kept a large sum of money stashed in the desk drawer of his study. That seemed a little unnecessary, since almost everything in the kingdom belonged to them, and the things that did not were purchased for him by his counselors and servants. She supposed he kept this stash for matters of foreign trade and wondered now why she had never thought to ask him. Whatever the reason, she wasn't complaining—this was exactly what she needed.

Emberlynn climbed out of bed and crept out of her room. Luckily, her father's study was in the same wing of the castle, just one floor below her bedchamber. She tiptoed to the servant's stair and climbed carefully down to the second floor.

When she reached his study she entered carefully, taking care not to disturb anything. She went straight to his bottom left drawer and pulled out one of numerous small bags of money. She opened it and quickly counted.

"*A hundred gold coins should be more than enough,*" she thought. "*Good.*"

With that, she went back to her room for the remainder of her sleepless night.

At first light Emberlynn was up and began setting her plan into motion. Although she had little appetite, she stopped by the kitchens and asked for a quick bite of fruit and some cheese on bread, to allay suspicion. Then she headed down to the stables. She went over her list one more time to make sure she hadn't forgotten anything: clothes—check, food—check, water—check, knife—check, map—check, flints—check... She had everything she should need packed neatly in the bag that was draped over her shoulder.

Emberlynn was dressed in her riding clothes. The only other person around the stables at this hour was Adam, the stable boy. It wasn't uncommon for Emberlynn to go for an early morning ride around the palace grounds on Artemis. She had it all planned out: she would let Adam see her leave and make him think it was just a short ride. Then she would ride as fast as she could to the nearest town where she would hitch a ride to Lemeth. She would send Artemis back to the castle, and when he returned rider-less, her father would think she had been either injured or taken hostage. By the time he sent the guard out looking for her, she would already be half way to Lemeth. If they did manage to catch up to her, she hoped that her disguise would be enough to keep her from being recognized.

"Good morning, Adam!" she said, as brightly as possible, as she reached the stables.

"Mornin', Miss," he replied cheerfully. "Off for yer mornin' ride, are ya?"

"Yup! Artemis deserves a nice ride. I haven't had a chance to take her out for an entire week, I was so busy with preparations for the ball."

"Ah, that she does!" Adam agreed.

He quickly saddled Artemis for Emberlynn, then headed to the barn to get food for the other horses.

When he was gone, she tied her bag to the saddle. Then she changed quickly into Margaret's pants and shirt and put her riding clothes in the bag. She didn't really want to take them with her, but she certainly couldn't stash them there. She was determined to leave behind no evidence. This had to work.

Emberlynn climbed onto Artemis' back and was off. They flew across the castle grounds and, in no time at all, were on their way to town. She knew Artemis was getting tired, but it was crucial she make good time; she had to be well away before anyone realized she was missing. When the princess was about half way to town, she stopped by a stream. She climbed off and let her horse drink while she put the finishing touches on her disguise.

She pulled the knife from her bag and looked at her reflection in a small pool of still water a few feet away from the stream. Using the pool as a mirror, she slowly and unwillingly began to cut her golden locks. It was painful for her to let go of something she prided herself on, but she made quick work of it. When she was done, Emberlynn took a step back and admired herself in the water. She had cut a bob that fell just above her shoulders. Though she mourned the loss of the beautiful long hair, she did think this new cut was cute on her. The princess kneeled down and got a small bit of mud on her hands which she put carelessly on her face and hair.

"*There!*" she thought, triumphantly, as she looked in the pool.

"*I look like a peasant, if I do say so myself.*"

She took the pile of hair she'd cut and burned it. She couldn't leave it lying there, looking suspicious. It smelled horrible, but at least it was out of her way. Then she climbed back on Artemis, who had now caught her breath, and was off again.

It took them hardly any time to reach Eiladuén, but it seemed like forever. She was so anxious that her plan wasn't going to work, but she'd come this far and wasn't about to turn back out of fear.

When she reached the edge of town, she climbed off Artemis and untied the bag from the saddle. Then she turned him to face the palace and gave him a hard pat on the rump, sending him trotting back home. He knew the way and Emberlynn was sure that, before long, he would make it safely home.

"Hopefully he'll go slowly and give me more time to get away."

Emberlynn mustered her courage walked confidently into town. Not many people were out and about yet and, luckily, no one had seen her ride up. Artemis was obviously a royal horse and the last thing she needed was to look more conspicuous than she already felt. She walked around town for a few minutes, looking for something that could be of aid to her.

Then she saw it. Parked in front of an old barn was a large wagon, loaded up with pigs. She tiptoed over to the barn and ducked behind the wagon.

"Don't be gone too long, Dear," came a voice from inside the barn.

"Well Laith is more than half way to Lemeth, Sweetheart. It'll take time to get there and back. But that's where we get the best price fer our animals."

This was all Emberlynn needed to hear. She climbed into the back of the cart, squeezing in between the pigs and burrowing into the straw.

"This is disgusting!" she thought. *"But I don't have many options."*

Then the voices spoke again.

"I know. I just hate ye being gone so long."

"Don't worry, I promise I'll be back in a few days. Ye'll hardly have time to miss me."

"We both know that ain't true," the woman laughed softly.

Emberlynn heard the man walk outside, climb onto the seat at the front of the cart, and settle in for the ride. He clicked his tongue and shook the reigns to encourage the old horse, who responded with a shiver of his mane before slowing starting forward. They were off.

CHAPTER 5

THE STOWAWAY

Emberlynn didn't know how long she had been cramped in the back of the small cart with the pack of filthy, smelly pigs, but finally she felt it come to a stop. She heard a new voice greeting the driver who, as far as she could tell, had stopped at the home of a friend for a midday meal. Her stomach growled loudly and she held her breath, hoping neither man had heard. After several tense moments had passed in silence, the men continued their conversation and the princess relaxed. She pulled out a bit of bread from her pack and, fighting off the greedy pigs, scarfed down a quick bite herself. Though she dozed off for a bit as the men headed inside to eat, it wasn't long before Emberlynn woke to the sound of the driver saying his goodbyes and felt the cart start up again. Several hours later, as the road was growing dark, they came to a halt a second time.

"I guess we've stopped for the night," she thought, quietly groaning as she sat up. Her whole body was stiff from the long journey. She began picking the straw out of her hair and thinking about what to do next. *"Well I know one thing for sure,"* she thought. *"I am not sleeping in the cart with the pigs."* Emberlynn turned her head and smelled her shoulder, shuddering as the

stench of pig filled her lungs. She had just begun climbing out of the cart to search for a more suitable bed when she heard a voice beside her in the darkness.

"Well I'll be!" it exclaimed.

Emberlynn turned to see the owner of the cart looking directly at her. She sat there, frozen, for a moment, unsure what to do. In her eagerness to leave the pigs being she had completely forgotten about him and hadn't thought that, of course, he would need to put the pigs up for the night.

"Idiot!" she scolded herself in her head.

"Looks like we've got ourselves a stowaway," he said, to no one in particular.

The princess slowly finished climbing out of the cart and tried to formulate a plan, an innocent grimace on her face.

The man held up his lantern so he could get a better look at Emberlynn.

"Goodness me, yer just a child," he said, shaking his head.

"Yes...I'm sorry..." Emberlynn said slowly, trying her best to formulate a plan. She knew she would have to make up a story sooner or later, so she may as well do it sooner.

"I know I shouldn't have...but... well, I'm trying to get to Lemeth and I heard you say you were going to Laith and..."

He looked at her sternly. "Runnin away from home are we?"

"No sir!" she exclaimed, quickly. "It's my brother..." she added, saying the first thing that came to mind. "Yes, my brother...Marcus... and I were going to Lemeth together to visit our...cousin...Felix...on his...birthday," she finshed, lamely.

OK, so maybe she was an only child and no one she knew was having a birthday, but it wasn't a complete lie. She did have a cousin that lived in Lemeth; she hadn't mentioned he was the prince, but still...

"If that's the case, where's yer brother?"

"We got separated."

The story started coming together in her head. She wouldn't say anything too far-fetched, but as long as she was telling stories, she may as well make them interesting.

"We live in Engeln, on the other side of the palace. We were traveling on horseback and we rode around the palace early this morning. Well, we passed the royal guard and they were really impressed by our horse, Emberlynn. We'd named her after the princess, ye see."

She suppressed a grin as she looked up at the man, trying to read his face. He seemed to be buying the story, because the stern look on his face had been replaced by one of interest. She felt herself relax and began to get more into the story. She even thought to throw in some colloquialisms, for effect, that she'd picked up from her servants.

"Yes, and they wanted to buy her from us but we said we wouldn't sell her, on account of our Pa raised her himself and she was one of the family. But the guards didn't take to kindly to being refused and they demanded we sell her. But Marcus didn't take too kindly to being ordered around and he sort of hit one of the guards who tried to take Emberlynn."

The man grimaced, imagining what would of course follow such an outburst.

"So, as you can imagine, that didn't go over too well. They beat Marcus pretty soundly and put him in the stocks for two whole days! And they took Emberlynn from me," she said, trying to sound both innocent and traumatized.

"Did they at least pay ye for her?" the man asked.

"Well, yes..." answered Emberlynn, pulling out the royal coin purse from her father's study. *That sure came in handy...* she thought.

"And Marcus?"

"Yes, poor Marcus. I wanted to stay with him, but he insisted I go on ahead so our cousin wouldn't worry about us. He's expecting us, ye see. And I did want to be there for his birthday. He's turning twenty, ye know. Anyway my brother said he would meet me in Lemeth at my cousin's once he'd been released. But I didn't have any other way to get there 'cause Emberlynn was our only horse. And I couldn't buy another one without Marcus or Father... I mean, Pa... so when I heard you saying you were going to Laith. It's on the way and all...and I just sort of climbed in. I'm sorry."

"Ah, you poor thing!" said the man.

Maybe her story had been a tad bit melodramatic, but he'd bought it, which was all she could ask for—especially since she wasn't a very good liar.

"I'd be happy to take you to Laith with me, Miss...?"

"Hannah," she said, quickly. She had no idea where that name had come from, but she liked it; it was pretty.

"Hannah," he repeated, holding out his hand. "I'm Ben. Pleasure."

She shook his hand and smiled. "Well, Ben... I really am sorry about sneaking on your cart."

"No matter," Ben replied. As I said, I'd be happy to take you with me. And you can help me care for my pigs."

"It's a deal. Thank you, Ben."

Once she had settled things with Ben, she was able to relax and take stock of the surroundings and her new acquaintance. She looked Ben over—he was a tall man with a kind face, who looked to be in his early forties. His thick head of hair was beginning to grey, and he had a short salt-and-pepper goatee on his very round face. She was thankful it was Ben's cart she has chosen to sneak onto because most people wouldn't have taken as kindly to stowaways. Then the princess turned and looked around; it was completely dark except for the circle of light cast from the lantern in Ben's hand. Emberlynn could just make out that the cart was parked next to a small barn.

Ben saw the curious look on her face.

"It's an inn for travelers," he explained.

"Well, actually this is the barn belonging to the inn. I can't stay in the inn itself what with my pigs and all. But they keep some cots set up in there for people like myself. Why don't ye let the pigs out of the cart and drive them into the barn while I go check in with the innkeeper?"

He pulled a second lantern from the front of the cart, which he lit and handed to Emberlynn. She thanked him and un-latched the back of the cart as Ben walked off into the darkness. The princess followed his instructions and awkwardly herded the pigs into the barn, locking them in an empty pen at the back. Ben returned as she was closing the gate, a small bag in his hands.

"Well, how about some shut-eye?" he asked, kindly. "I reckon being a stowaway takes it out of ye," he laughed.

She smiled at his kindness and laughed at his comment. Then she let out a gigantic yawn.

"I'll take that as a yes."

Emberlynn nodded.

"I'll take this cot here, by the pig pen. Why don't you make yerself comfortable up in the loft. There should be one up there as well."

"Thanks," she replied, climbing the ladder up to the loft.

There she found a small cot, as Ben had predicted.

"This looks great," she called down.

Again, her words weren't entirely true. She had grown up in the palace of Ardia and slept in the most luxurious bed money could buy. Both she and the barn smelled like pigs and the cot was small and lumpy. The sheets were torn, and the once-white pillow was a dingy shade of grey. But then again, anything would seem comfortable after the spending the day in the back of a pig cart.

"Sleep well, then. I'll wake ye in the morning when I'm ready to leave. But I should warn ye, I like to get an early start."

"That's OK, I'm an earlier riser!" This, at least, was the truth.

The princess climbed into bed and snuggled down under the covers. Evenings were chilly in Ardia, even during the spring. She was sore, cold, and hungry.

"Oh no, I've forgotten to eat supper!" she thought.

Her hands fumbled for her bag at the foot of the cot. She finally found it, pulling out one of the loaves of bread she'd packed. She tore a piece off the end and shoved it in her mouth. Three small loaves of bread—that was the only food she had, and it had to last her at least 'til she reached Lemeth. So she ate her small ration, took a small draught from her canteen, then tied her bag back up and lay down for a very interesting night's sleep. All things considered, she considered herself fortunate; Ben had believed her story and was taking her as far as Laith. She didn't know what she was going to do from there, but she would figure that out when the time came. For now, she had money, a little food, and a place to sleep. And, above all, she never again had to climb into the back of a pig cart.

It seemed she had been right about one thing: her eighteenth birthday had marked the beginning of her adventure. It wasn't the one she had expected, but she couldn't say it wouldn't be exciting. She couldn't wait to see where it would take her.

Emberlynn let out a sigh, closed her eyes, and ran her fingers absentmindedly over the key around her neck. Then she drifted into a deep, dreamless sleep.

Back at the palace, things were not so peaceful. Artemis had returned just before lunchtime, rider-less.

This wasn't entirely uncommon for Emberlynn, as she had been known to leave her horse to graze while she took a walk in the gardens. Therefore, the king and queen didn't think much of it. But when she didn't show up at lunch they began to worry.

"Margaret!" called the queen.

"Yes, Your Highness?" Margaret answered as she hurried to the table.

"Go upstairs to the princess' room and see if she has perhaps returned without our knowledge."

"Of course."

Margaret hurried upstairs to Emberlynn's room. She gently knocked on the door a few times before entering. Emberlynn wasn't there, but Margaret did notice an envelope on her bed, addressed to the king. Letter in hand, she ran downstairs as quickly as possible, entering the dining room a little short of breath.

"There's no sign of her, but I found this in her room," she said, handing the envelope to the king.

He opened it to reveal the following, scribbled on the royal stationary:

Father,

I went to Westin Abbey to visit Banning's father.
You can expect my return sometime this afternoon.

Emberlynn

"Ah, she's merely gone to visit Duke Theron. Very well, let us finish our meal in peace," said the king.

They went about their day as they would have any other. The king had his morning audience with the subjects that had come seeking his help and advice. The queen saw to the affairs of the palace and had a fitting for a new gown she had ordered. It wasn't until supper had ended with no sign of Emberlynn that they began to worry once more.

"Night is falling and it will be dark soon," noted the queen. "Perhaps we should send a carriage for Emberlynn."

The king agreed, and Margaret was sent, along with a royal carriage, to accompany the princess back to the palace.

An hour had passed and Margaret and the princess had still not returned. The queen began pacing in the throne room as the king sat anxiously on his throne.

"What could be taking them so long?" she asked. "Emberlynn's never disappeared for an entire day like this."

Just then there was a loud pounding on the door of the throne room and the Duke came bursting in.

"Your Majesty!" he exclaimed, alarm evident on his face. "I'm told Emberlynn set out to visit me this morning. But I must tell you, she never arrived at Westin Abbey."

The king stood up suddenly and crossed the room 'til he was standing next to the Duke.

"You mean to tell me my daughter has not been with you today?!" he asked, terror rising in his voice with each word.

"No, Sire, I haven't seen her since the ball last night."

The queen let out a cry and ran to her husband.

"Our daughter!" she cried. "Our daughter is missing!!!"

They all took in the weight of those words, then panic began to set in. After a moment of stunned silence, the king hastened from the throne room, the other two in tow.

"ANTONY!!" he bellowed, beckoning the head of the royal guard. "Someone get me Antony!!!"

There was a loud commotion as all the servants scurried around the palace in search of Antony. A few minutes later a tall, stocky man in his late thirties came running into the corridor.

"Antony!" said the king. "Princess Emberlynn is missing! She left early this morning to ride to Westin Abbey, but she never arrived. Artemis returned alone and...my daughter is gone!" he exclaimed.

"Sir," Antony replied. "I'll send half the guard out immediately in search of her!" He set out to give the order when the king called after him.

"Please, keep this from the public as long as possible. When they find out Emberlynn is missing there will be chaos in the kingdom."

"Of course sir," he called back. With that he was off, along with half the royal guard, in search of the princess.

"It'll be all right, Gwyneria," the king whispered to his wife. "We'll find her."

CHAPTER 6

RUMOURS AND LIES

The next morning Emberlynn woke in a strange, dimly lit room. A few rays of light had forced their way bravely through the small cracks in the wooden planks which formed the walls. She rolled over in bed and...*THUD!*

"Ow!" Emberlynn groaned.

The princess had rolled right off the edge of the small cot. It was then, as she sat on the floor rubbing her tired eyes, that Emberlynn remembered where she was.

"Everything okay up there?" called Ben.

"Yeah..." she said slowly, picking herself up. "Everything's fine."

"Well I'm glad ye're up 'cause I was just about to wake ye. I've loaded the pigs and I'm all ready to set out—after breakfast, of course."

At the mention of food, Emberlynn's stomach growled. She had eaten nothing but that small portion of bread the day before.

"Breakfast?" the princess asked, as she grabbed her bag and carefully descended the ladder from the loft.

"Yeah, I bought a few eggs from the main house of the inn. I imagine ye're hungry after the day ye had yesterday. And I never set out on an empty stomach. So dig in and let's hit the road."

Emberlynn eyed the eggs with desire but said, "I couldn't possibly take your food. You've been so kind in letting me stay here and taking me to Laith with you. Besides, I have some bread."

At this she held up her backpack.

"Nonsense," he replied. I bought more than I can eat myself so if ye don't help me, I'll just have to throw 'em out."

Her stomach growled again, audibly this time.

Ben gave her a look that told her she'd lost the argument, so she grinned, grabbing the plate he held out for her.

"Thanks."

The pair quickly gulped down their breakfast and were back on the road in no time. Emberlynn was much more comfortable riding in the front with Ben than she had been the previous day; she laughed at how poorly planned her attempt at being a stowaway had proved.

"What?" Ben asked, in question to her sudden laughter.

"Nothing. It just smells a whole lot better up here," she said with a grin.

"I imagine so," Ben chuckled. "Well I'm glad ye're comfortable because Laith is another day and a half's ride from here."

The day was pretty uneventful. At one point the cart got stuck in a bit of mud, so Ben let Emberlynn drive while he pushed from behind. Fortunately, they were able to get it out without losing too much time. Once again, they reached the inn at nightfall. It was a similar setup to the previous inn, with Ben and Emberlynn sleeping in the barn with the pigs. Once they were unloaded and penned up for the night, Emberlynn climbed the ladder to the loft and curled up in the small cot, falling quickly to sleep.

It wasn't until the final day of their journey that things began to get a little more interesting.

⁀

Antony returned to the palace the next morning to check in with the king and queen.

"I'm sorry, but we haven't found any sign of her," he said, sadly.

"We did find hoof tracks leading toward the village, but they disappear just past the river, where the grass begins."

The king and queen had been up all night, waiting and hoping for news of their daughter. Antony's heart fell as he looked into their tired eyes. While they may not be particularly close to their daughter, but everyone knew they loved her.

"Thank you, Antony," said the king, quietly.

"My men are still out searching. I've sent them to all the neighboring villages. I'm leaving shortly to rejoin them. I just wanted to update you."

"Please send word if you find anything at all."

"Of course, Sire. In the meantime, may I suggest Your Highnesses get some rest? We're doing everything in our power to find Princess Emberlynn. I've even sent out another group of the guard. Everyone that's not guarding the palace is out in the search."

With that, he departed to join the search party. The day passed with nothing to report until just before nightfall, when Antony dispatched this letter to the king:

Your Majesty,
We tried to conceal the reason for our search from your subjects.
However there were lots of questions as to why half the
guard was out searching the villages.
I'm afraid someone has leaked the news about
the Princess' disappearance—
Probably one of the younger members of the guard who
didn't understand the need for discretion.
As you can imagine, it is all the people are talking about.
Antony

It started just like the previous morning: they woke early, loaded the pigs in the cart, and shared a quick breakfast. Emberlynn had only one loaf of bread left, as she had shared the others with Ben in return for more eggs and a little venison he'd bought from the second inn.

"I'm going to run out for a few minutes to buy a few more loaves of bread before we leave. I saw a Baker's shop down the street a little way," Emberlynn called to Ben.

"Okay, I'll sign out with the innkeeper and double-check the cart."

Emberlynn strolled down the street to the Baker's shop and had almost reached it when she spotted something that made her heart stand still. There were two men standing in front of the shop, talking to the little old man who owned it. They were clad in dark green jackets, with ivory sashes adorned with medals and ribbons; members of the royal guard.

The princess dove quickly behind a neighboring building and held her breath. As the guards finished their conversation with the Baker, they headed down the street in the direction Emberlynn was hiding.

She knew that she was well disguised and the odds of them recognizing her were slim, but she wasn't willing to take any chances. She crouched down, flattened herself against the side of the building, and tried her hardest to be invisible. Emberlynn waited with bated breath until she heard them enter the shop. Then she ran as quickly as her legs could carry her back to Ben and the safety of his cart.

"Whoa, what's the hurry?" Ben asked as Emberlynn ran up to the cart breathing heavily.

"Nothing," she gasped. "Just, we should leave now if we want to make it to Laith before lunch."

"Yeah, Okay..." Ben replied, looking a little suspicious. "So, where's yer bread?"

"They were...out."

"Out? First thing in the morning? I'd have thought they'd have just put out some fresh loaves."

"Nope...out."

"Okay. Well in that case, I guess we'll be on our way to Laith."

"Good, let's go!" she agreed, jumping on the cart trying to look inconspicuous.

Ben climbed up next to Emberlynn and they were off. They passed another group of guards on their way out of the village but, luckily, they didn't pay any attention to a pair of tattered travelers.

"Aye, I didn't tell ye..." began Ben.

"Tell me what?"

"I asked the innkeeper what was up with all the green-coats, and he told me they're out looking for Princess Emberlynn. It turns out she's missing!"

Emberlynn's face froze in fear. She took a deep breath, praying that Ban hadn't noticed the panic on her face, and tried to sound disinterested.

"Do they have any idea what happened to her?" she asked, faking calmness.

"She disappeared while riding just outside the palace grounds. They suspect she was kidnapped."

The princess let out a silent sigh of relief.

"Wow, that's terrible. Who would kidnap the princess?"

"That's what everyone's wondering. They haven't the foggiest. And that's why they're out lookin', and askin' around. Hopin' to find a lead or a bit of information that may help 'em."

"Hmmm..."

"Good," Emberlynn thought.

"It hasn't even crossed their minds that I've run away. And they don't have any leads. Unfortunately, they're out looking for me now so I'm going to have to be on my guard. And hopefully I'll do a better job at sneaking around than I did with Ben and the pigs."

It was then that Emberlynn realized how very little she knew about Ben. She had told him a fake story about her life, but at least it was a story.

"So, tell me about your wife..."she said.

"Oh, she's an amazing woman..."

Ben went on to tell her about his wife, their life on the farm together, and other such things. Emberlynn was more than happy to listen to it. They had a fairly long ride ahead of them, and it gave her something interesting to do without having to come up with more fake stories from her pretend life.

CHAPTER 7

A DOOR TO NOWHERE

Evening fell as the pair pulled into Laith. As they would be going their separate ways the next day, Ben back home to his wife and Emberlynn to Lemeth "to visit her cousin," they decided to have dinner together in a local pub.

"I like to go out with a bang," Ben told her "so it's my treat."

"I couldn't possibly!" Emberlynn protested.

"Nonsense, Hannah!" He retorted. "Ye've done me a favor, ye have, helping me look after my pigs."

"And ye've done me a favor," she imitated "by allowing me to ride in your cart and sleep in the stable with you and your pigs. Really I couldn't."

After a bit more protesting, Ben managed to buy dinner and Emberlynn thanked him profusely. Then they returned to the barn and settled in for the night. Despite the hard cots in the stable lofts, the princess had no trouble falling asleep; she was exhausted from the journey and unaccustomed to spending so much time outdoors in the heat. Her eyes closed the second they hit the pillow and she was out.

Sometime later she woke with a start to the sound of knocking. The princess sat up and tried to get her bearings. Beneath her she felt the cool touch of marble floor—it reminded her of when she was a child crawling around the palace. The thought made her smile. That smile quickly faded, however, as Emberlynn realized there shouldn't be any marble in the loft of a barn.

She stood up quickly, her pulse racing.

"Ben?" she said quietly.

"Ben?" A little louder this time.

Emberlynn began turning in circles.

"Where am I?" she asked no one in particular.

The princess strained her eyes in the darkness, hoping to make out more of her surroundings. Then she heard the knocking sound again. She froze.

"Hello?" called Emberlynn, tentatively. "Who's there?"

She walked instinctively in the direction of the sound, but before she realized what was happening, she had walked straight into a marble wall.

"Okay, oww!" she winced, putting her hand gingerly on her throbbing forehead.

Emberlynn shook off the stunned feeling and slowly found the wall once more, continuing her search for the source of the sound. Suddenly her hands found something that wasn't marble. Metal, maybe? The knocking got louder. She ran her fingers along it carefully, feeling the patterns on the surface. The princess stopped when she felt something protruding from the mysterious metal surface. It was long and thin—a door handle?

Emberlynn took a step back, squinting into the darkness. Her eyes had adjusted just enough to allow her to make out the shape of the door. She couldn't see any of the details, though, and that frustrated her. Where was she? Where did this door lead? And where, for the love of Ardia, were the candles in this place?

Knock, knock, knock.

"Hello?" answered the princess.

Knock, knock.

"Hello? My name is Emb—um, Hannah. Can you hear me?"

Knock, knock, knock, knock.

She walked determinedly to the door, this time without hitting her head, grabbed the handle, and pulled as hard as she could. Nothing. She tried to turn it any and every which way. Still nothing. She put all her weight on it and tried to force it open. That didn't work either.

Eventually Emberlynn gave up, took a step back again, and sat cross-legged on the floor.

The knocking had stopped and there she was, alone in a marble room in terrifying silence.

Thud.

"Oof!" she cried, as the wind was knocked out of her body. "Ouch!"

Emberlynn opened her eyes and was blinded by the sunlight streaming into...the barn loft?

She was sprawled on the floor next to her cot, sheets strewn everywhere.

"Morning, Hannah!" came a voice from below. "Did ye fall out of bed again?"

"It would appear so," the princess called down.

Ben laughed.

"I guess...I must have been dreaming," she whispered to herself.

"What an odd dream."

Emberlynn put the sheets back on the bed, threw her things together, then climbed the ladder down to the ground floor of the barn. As he had the past few days, Ben had gotten breakfast—this time from the local bakery. Emberlynn sat down and ate hungrily.

"Slow down, before ye choke yerself," Ben laughed. "And, wait...what happened to yer head?"

Emberlynn looked at him inquisitively. "Nothing that I know of."

She grabbed the spoon she was eating with and studied her reflection. There was a distinct bruise forming on her forehead.

"I must have hit my head just now when I fell off the cot."

"I'm not sure a bruise like that could form this quickly. Mayhaps ye hit it on something yesterday?"

"I don't recall doing so, but I suppose...unless...no. No, it couldn't be."

"Unless what?"

"Nothing. I just...I must have banged my head when I was letting the pigs out last night."

Ben watched as she studied her reflection in the spoon, and he had a feeling she was hiding something. No need to press the matter, though. He smiled and shrugged.

"Ye've gotta learn to be more careful, girl."

The princess chuckled. But she couldn't help but think, as she looked at her reflection, that the bruise had formed in the exact place she had hit when she walked into the marble wall.

"Impossible," Emberlynn told herself.

She must have hit her head pretty hard on...whatever it was she hit...to think something so absurd, even briefly.

After breakfast the two companions said their goodbyes.

"Thank you so much for letting me travel with you, Ben," Emberlynn told him, shaking his hand.

"Tis' been a pleasure, Miss Hannah. Best of luck with yer visit to yer cousin. Be safe, now."

"I will," she promised, smiling.

At this they parted company. Ben loaded up his pigs, climbed up on his cart and headed to the market in the center of town. Emberlynn waved to him as he left, then she turned around and gathered her bearings. She pulled out her map and located Laith.

"*Ok, Ember*" she told herself.

"*You are a two day ride from here. You don't have a carriage. Or a cart. Or a horse. Great. Looks like you're walking. So you'll get there in...never.*"

She sighed and stared into the early morning sun.

"*That's East. So thaaaaat's...south,*" she said as she turned slightly to the right.

"*And that's the way I need to go.*"

The princess stashed her map back in her bag and set off. She had been walking for just five minutes, and hadn't yet reached the town center, when it happened. The townspeople were up and headed to the morning market, crowding the streets. Emberlynn didn't have any time to waste, so she turned down an alleyway which appeared to be a shortcut. She didn't even see it coming. She was walking past a small grove of trees when two men jumped out and ambushed her. Emberlynn tried to fight them, but it was no use; they were much stronger than she was, and there were two of them. They knocked her down into the mud and ripped her bag from her hands. One of the men stepped closer and reached down toward her. The princess kicked him in the shin and backed away; he fell to the ground, gasping in pain.

"Don't touch me!" Emberlynn said, indignantly.

"Well, well..." said the man who was still standing. "We got ourselves a feisty one, Charles."

The man Emberlynn had kicked, whom she assumed was Charles, picked himself up and glared at her.

"What should we do with her?" questioned the first man, eyeing her up and down. Then he whistled.

Emberlynn stared back at them, a fire forming in her eyes.

"I am a lady, and I will be treated as such," she demanded, standing up shakily and brushing the dirt off her clothes.

"Beggin' yer pardon, miss," cackled Charles, patronizingly. "But I think we'll be the ones givin' orders 'round here."

He stepped closer to her again.

Emberlynn began to panic. What would these savages do with her? As Charles reached for her again, she did the only thing she could think of—she punched him square in the jaw.

Charles looked at her, stunned, and wiped a trickle of blood from his mouth.

Emberlynn clenched her hand, which was throbbing, but refused to show any sign of pain.

The two bandits backed away and the first man said, "Let's get out of here, Charles. She's not worth it. Besides," he added, lifting her bag, "we already got what we wanted."

The pair turned around and walked quickly away, disappearing into the shadows. Once she was sure they were gone, Emberlynn collapsed to the ground, shaking violently. She wrapped her arms around her knees and wept. She had just been threatened by two horrible men. She didn't even want to think about what might have happened had she not hit Charles. For that alone she knew she was lucky. But the truth was, she was alone in a strange city. Her happiness depended on her reaching Lemeth without being found. And she now had no food, no change of clothes, and no money. They had taken everything.

After a few minutes, she took a deep breath and wiped her eyes on her tattered sleeve.

"Maybe I should just give up and go home," she thought.

"I could go back to the palace and have a nice big meal, and a hot bath. And I could sleep somewhere that doesn't smell like pigs. And...and...I could be miserable for the rest of my life."

Sher eyes filled with tears once more.

"I don't have time for this," she scolded herself.

Emberlynn took another calming breath and leaned back. Her right hand landed on something hard and metal. She turned around to examine the object—it was her royal signet ring. The princess picked it up, wiped the mud off it with the last clean patch of her shirt, and held it close to her heart. This one small token gave her hope again. They might have taken her clothes, food, money, map, tools...and just about all the things you need to survive on the road, but they hadn't gotten everything. This ring was her identity. Even if no one else knew it, she still had her signet ring to remind her of who she was and where she'd come from. And they hadn't taken her courage and drive. She would not be forced to marry against her will. She was not any man's property to be given away without her consent. She would make it to Lemeth. She just wasn't sure how yet.

Emberlynn unhooked the chain holding the key, slipped the ring on beside it, fastened the clasp, and stuffed both items back beneath her clothes. Her two most precious possessions. Her only two possessions. She knew time was of the essence and was quickly running out. She had to get going.

The princess decided the first thing she needed was food. She didn't have any money to buy it, but the whole country belonged to her family so she supposed it wouldn't technically be stealing. Emberlynn stopped by a small creek on her way to the city center to wash off some of the mud. Then she went straight to the market without taking any more shortcuts.

When she got there, she staked out the merchant booths. Her plan was to hit one of the outlying ones, so there would be less chance of getting caught. She should have realized that she was notoriously bad at sneaking, but that was a fact she remembered far too late. So late, in fact, that she was already locked in the stocks in the town square before it sank in.

"*A whole day in here?*" she thought, trying not to start crying again. "

This has so not been a good morning. I don't have time for this. I have to be on my way to Lemeth. And, oh my gosh, what if someone sees me here and recognizes me?! They'll take me back to the palace. Oh dear..."

"What on earth are you doing there, young lady?!" Emberlynn heard a man's voice exclaim.

"*Oh dear. Oh dear, oh dear, oh dear...*"

She looked up and saw Ben standing in front of her.

"Hannah, it hasn't even been an hour since I left you, and you're already in the stocks."

He shook his head.

The guard walked up and said, "I'll have to ask you to step away now, mister."

Luckily Ben was quick on his feet.

"I'm sorry, sir. Ya see, this is my daughter, Hannah. We're here in town selling our pigs. We get the best prices for 'em here. I brought this one with me..."

At this is motioned toward Emberlynn.

" ...'Cause I hoped to keep her out of trouble for a bit. Guess not, though. Young lady, you are in so much trouble!"

"Sorry...Dad," Emberlynn said, looking truly guilty.

The guard sighed. "I'll let her off with a warning this time. But you really must keep a better eye on your daughter. And don't let me catch her around here again, ya hear me?"

"Yes sir," they said, in unison.

The guard released Emberlynn from the stocks, and Ben led her away from the market and back to his cart.

"What was that about?" he asked her on the way.

Emberlynn told him the whole story. Well...the whole story minus the part about her signet ring—she didn't think he needed that particular detail. But she told him how they'd knocked her down and taken her bag, and how she'd punched Charles when he approached her. Emberlynn also told him how she'd found herself with no money for food and no idea what to do next.

Ben whistled loudly. "Quite a story there. Well, I'm glad they left when they did. And I'm glad I ran into ye back at the stocks."

"Me, too. And thank you so much for getting that guard to let me go. I don't know what I would have done without you."

"Well I know what ye're doing now," said Ben, flatly.

"Staying in Laith until I can find some money and figure out a way to get myself to Lemeth?"

"Getting yer rear end up on this cart."

"But Ben," Emberlynn protested. "I can't go home, I just can't! I mean..." she caught herself. "I just can't miss my cousin's birthday. I promised him I'd be there. Please don't take me back home."

"The thought never crossed my mind. No, young lady, I am taking ye to Lemeth."

"That's so kind of you, but I couldn't ask you to do that."

"Well ye didn't ask."

"Yes, but, Ben, you promised your wife you'd be back soon. She'll be worried sick."

"Nonsense, I'll just write her a letter and explain. She's a gracious woman. She'll understand. Now sit."

Emberlynn knew the matter was decided, so she climbed up on the cart and waited for Ben as he ran to the postal station and sent a letter to his wife, Sarah. Before long he returned and they headed off toward Lemeth.

The second stage of their journey was much like the first, only this time they were able to stay inside the inns, as they no longer had the pigs. Ben rented two rooms each night, and made sure Hannah was good and fed. And he kept a much closer eye on her than before.

Before they knew it, they had reached Lemeth. The border lay at the top of a great hill, and Emberlynn felt a rush of excitement as she looked down into the valley. She could see for miles, and the view was breathtaking.

"Beautiful, ain't it?" said Ben.

"Beautiful," Emberlynn chorused, at peace for the first time since she'd left the palace.

CHAPTER 8

SHADOWS OF THE PAST

Back in Adria, it was utter chaos. King Edric and Queen Gwyneria were doing their best to keep a brave face for the people. But behind closed doors, they were a complete wreck. Neither had slept much since their daughter's disappearance, and the queen was hardly eating.

"I know you have high hopes of finding her, Edric," said the queen, "but it's been a week. An entire week. Where could she be? I'm beginning to fear the worst."

"I can send out more troops for the search party," he replied, quietly. "Other than that, I'm not sure what I can do?"

"Maybe it's time we got the people involved; offered a reward if she is found."

"Margaret!" the King called loudly.

"Yes, Your Highness?" she said, scrambling into the room and bowing.

"See if you can track down Antony. I have another job for him."

❧

It was all anyone in Ardia could talk about.

"Have you heard? The royal family has issued a reward for the findin' of the princess. 730 Ryns!"

"For that amount, whoever took her must be runnin' hasty to the palace."

"Wouldn't they be thrown in the dungeon for kidnappin'?"

"Naw, if'n it were me, I'd say I'd saved her—maybe found her in a ditch or sum'n."

"Wonder if she'll turn up soon..."

⁂

Emberlynn stood motionless, staring out into the distance. It had been years since she'd last visited her uncle, and she couldn't remember anything from that trip. She hopped down off the cart and took in the view; her whole body tingled as she took her first, tentative, steps down the hill, across the border, and into the kingdom of Lemeth.

"Race you down the hill!" she shouted to Ben, grinning mischievously.

Then she was off. Emberlynn ran as quickly as her legs could carry her. She felt like a doe, racing across the open space—almost as if she could fly. Then Emberlynn did something she hadn't done in years—she threw caution to the wind and dived headfirst down the hill, rolling the rest of the way down in a fit of laughter.

"Come on, slowpoke!" she called back to Ben, who was still just over halfway down.

"Hey now, I've got a horse and a cart to worry about. Ye've only got yerself," he laughed.

She stood up, brushed herself off, and took in the moment. Standing there, on the outskirts of Lemeth, she felt empowered.

She felt alive. She felt...free. And she was. She had crossed the border into freedom. Away from obligation. Away from duty. Away from people trying to live her life for her. From now on, her life could be anything she wanted it to be. And that was a wonderful and terrifying thought.

"Come on, Hannah" called Ben, finally reaching the bottom of the hill. "If we make good time, we can reach the first town by nightfall."

Emberlynn climbed back onto the cart and the pair headed for town.

Faryn. The name popped into Emberlynn's head suddenly.

"The first town you reach in Lemeth after leaving Ardia is Faryn," she whispered.

"What's that?" asked Ben.

"Oh, nothing. I was just talking to myself."

"*Faryn,*" she thought. "*Maybe I remember more about this place than I thought. Or maybe I will once I reach it...*"

⁋

"Where could she be?" Banning asked his father.

The pair was sitting around the table in the great hall of Westin Abbey. Banning had returned as soon as he heard the news about Emberlynn's disappearance.

A servant had just arrived with the main course of their evening meal. He placed a large roasted pig on the table and turned to the Duke.

"Can I get you anything else, Your Grace?"

"No, that will be all. Thank you, ever so much, Marshall. Please return once the dessert course is ready to be served."

The servant bowed and headed back to the kitchen.

"Does he seem a little creepy to you?" Marshall whispered to a passing maid.

"What do you mean?"

"Those two are always so...nice. Way more than is normal for a noble."

"Well I guess it makes sense when you think about it."

"What do you mean?"

"Duke Theron wasn't born a Lemethian noble. Didn't you know?"

"No...wait, how did that happen?"

"No one knows for sure, but he did some sort of service for the king I think."

At that moment, a few other servants came down the hallway.

"We're not supposed to talk about it," she mouthed. "The Duke doesn't want people knowing he's not blood noble."

Marshall nodded, still a bit confused.

"Thanks, Georgia," he whispered.

Georgia greeted the other servants while Marshall returned to the kitchen to finish the dessert course. When the pudding was ready, he loaded it onto a tray and headed back to the great hall. He was about to enter when he heard hushed voices from the other side of the door.

"Honestly, Father. She's been gone for over a week. We could have finished most of the preparations for our wedding by now."

"Patience, my boy. King Edric has just issued a very generous reward for her safe return. Enough to entice even the hardest of criminals. Whoever has her...they'll bring her back. Unless..."

"Unless what, Father?"

"Banning. Are you absolutely certain she loves you?"

"Positive. She was completely and irreversibly smitten. Except..."

"Except?"

"Well, that night at the ball. Emberlynn was acting strange."

"How so?"

"She...hesitated. When I asked her to marry me. For a moment I thought she might actually say no. Nonsense of course."

"Banning!" the Duke exclaimed, sternly. "Why did you not mention this before?"

"I hardly thought it important, Father. She's obviously in love with me. And...well, look at me. I think it was just some strange female emotional nonsense. She came to her senses after a minute or two."

"That's not the point, Son."

"Then tell me, Father. What is this elusive point?"

"The point is...what if she wasn't kidnapped?"

Marshall's eyes widened from outside the door.

"You aren't suggesting...?"

"It was just a thought, Banning. But for now we shall sit back and wait. Perhaps she will turn up now that the King has offered such a notable reward. Yes, son, now we wait, and enjoy our pudding...which really should be here by now."

"Marshall!" the Duke called. "Have you finished the dessert course yet?"

Marshall took a deep breath and opened the door.

"Here you are, Your Grace! Sorry for the delay."

He set the tray down on the table.

"No apologies needed, Marshall," said Theron, grinning. Thank you for the pudding. It looks delightful."

Marshall nodded, and swiftly left the room.

"First of all," thought Marshall, *"blood noble or not, that guy is way too nice. And secondly, what did he mean about Princess*

Emberlynn. If she wasn't kidnapped then that means she ran away. Surely he doesn't think... But then again, if she hesitated to accept Banning's proposal maybe she didn't want to marry him. And she must have had a reason. Besides his family's over-whelming creepiness..."

Chapter 9

HANNAH AND FELIX

Ben and Emberlynn pulled into Faryn just before nightfall. They checked into a quaint little inn on the outskirts of the town and, after a quick dinner at the pub downstairs, said their goodnights and retired to their respective rooms.

As she sat by the window looking out over the town, Emberlynn was struck by its simple beauty. The sun had set and every building, as far as the eye could see, was dotted with lanterns. It was almost like the star-line began at the ground and continued all the way into heavens; as if the sky itself were on fire, exploding into millions of tiny sparks.

Emberlynn let out a deep, peaceful sigh. Then she closed the curtains and curled up in her cozy little bed. It was nothing compared to her room at the palace, with its lavish silks and oversized cushy bed, but after a week of sleeping on a cot in various barns, she was quite comfortable. Emberlynn blew out her candle and drifted easily off to sleep.

The next thing Emberlynn knew she found herself, once more, lying in the dark on a cold marble floor. She took a few determined breaths before standing up and making her way across the room. After shuffling cautiously for a minute, her hands finally felt the cool sting of the marble wall. Emberlynn felt her way along the wall, searching for the door she'd found a few nights prior. Nothing. She was growing increasingly frustrated until she heard a slow familiar knock coming from the other side of the room.

"Great," she announced to no one in particular. "Now I just have to find my way back across the room without tripping over anything or running into anymore walls."

She touched her forehead gently and winced. The bruise was fading, but it was still a little sore from the last time she'd been here.

"What does a girl have to do to get some light in here?" she asked the darkness.

Suddenly a blinding light came out of the darkness, as if by magic. Emberlynn turned around to see a beautiful chandelier hanging in the very center of the room, lit by hundreds of white candles. She squinted, shielding her eyes from the unexpected brightness. Then she blinked a few times. Once her eyes adjusted to the light, she found herself standing in a huge marble hall. She stared at it for a moment, barely breathing.

Emberlynn was pulled out of her trance when the knocking started up again. She whirled around, and all the breath left her body.

In the very middle of a white marble wall, centered between two giant columns, was a large silver door. But that doesn't do it justice. It was immense and immaculate; there wasn't a single speck or smudge on to be seen. A maze of intricate designs and pictures was cast into it. Staring at it made Emberlynn feel a little dizzy. It shone so brilliantly it almost seemed like had its own light source, as if the silver had been cast with fairy dust.

She walked slowly over to the door and placed a tentative hand on it. It was definitely the same door she had felt previously—the handle was the same, and she remembered the feeling of the strange designs. The closer she looked, the more sure she became that there was some sort of magic to this door. Emberlynn leaned in closer and sneezed. She stepped back, scratched her nose, and scrunched up her face.

"The effects of a sudden bright light," she thought.

Emberlynn shook her head and took a deep breath. Then she closed her eyes and pressed her palm firmly against the door.

Knock, knock.

Her eyes flew open. She felt a strange tingling in her hand. Suddenly the door shone a little brighter as tiny points of light began to swirl through the designs. Emberlynn gasped.

"It was cast with fairy dust! But I've never seen anything...I mean...it's impossible to get and...fairies don't..." she trailed off.

Knock.

Knock, knock, knock.

Emberlynn pulled on the handle of the door, trying desperately to open it. After a few minutes she gave up. At this point she managed to pull her attention away from the door and to the rest of the room. Something she had failed to notice earlier was its overwhelming emptiness. Besides the door and several marble columns, there was absolutely nothing in the room—no windows, no furniture...nothing but the chandelier. It was a little unsettling.

Having nothing else to do, Emberlynn sat down in the middle of the floor and stared at the door. She studied the patterns and pictures as the fairy dust slowly settled back down, returning the door to its original faint gleam.

Knock, Knock, Knock.

Emberlynn groaned.

Knock, knock.

"Hannah?"came a familiar voice.

Emberlynn sat up with a start and found herself back in her bed at the inn, the sun already high in the sky. It was then she noticed a strange tingling in her hand.

"*I must have slept on it, and it fell asleep,*" she told herself. "*You are a silly one these days, Ember.*"

Knock, knock.

"Hannah? Are ye in there?"

She rubbed her eyes, swung herself out of bed, and opened the door with a yawn.

"Good morning, sleepy head," said Ben, chuckling. "A bit of a late riser today, are we?"

"Sorry about that," she replied, sheepishly. "I was having the strangest dream."

"Well ye've had a rougher week than ye're used to, I reckon. That little frame of yer's needed the rest. I was just stopping by to say that I'm headed to breakfast, and do ye want to join me?"

"Of course. Just give me a moment to wash up a bit."

Ben nodded. "I'll be in my room next door when ye're done," he said, smiling.

She closed the door and surveyed herself in the mirror. She was a mess. She had lost everything but the clothes on her back when Charles and his buddy attacked her. She had been traveling and sleeping in her one pair of clothes, and they were in pretty poor shape. They were splattered in dried mud, smelled awful, and were beginning to tear. Her hair had mats in a few places, and pieces were sticking up on top of her head.

There was a basin of cool water that had been placed in her room the night before for drinking and washing. She took a sip and savored the way it felt running down her dry throat. Then she splashed some on her face and scrubbed the dirt off it, wiping it on the cloth next to the basin. She stared at her reflection and cringed. This small bowl of water wasn't nearly enough to do any proper washing, and this inn didn't have a bath. Her first order of business when she got...wherever it was she was going... was to find either a river or an inn with a bath and get good and clean. She turned her head and sniffed herself.

Cough. Cough, cough.

She smelled very strongly of pig and...*sniff*...outside.

Cough.

The thought of a bath lifted her spirits, and she began whistling as she headed down to breakfast with Ben. The pair sat across the table from each other, munching on some toast with apricot jam.

"So," asked Ben, wiping some crumbs out of his beard.

"Where is it in Lemeth that yer cousin lives? I've come this far and I don't want ye endin' up in the stocks again..."

It was only then that Emberlynn realized she had no idea where she was going, much less how she was going to convince Ben to leave her there without raising too much suspicion.

"He lives here in Faryn, actually," she replied, after a few moments' thought.

"Well I left ye in Laith, and didn't even get out of town before ye'd gotten yerself in trouble. So this time I'm taking ye straight to yer cousin's house."

"That's sweet of you, Ben, but really not necessary. I'm sure I can find my uncle and auntie's from here."

"I'm sure ye can, but I'm not leavin' 'til ye're safely with yer family."

It was hard to be irritated with such a sweet and generous man.

"Thank you," she said, smiling. "We can head there after we finish breakfast."

She would just have to figure out some way to ditch him in town. Emberlynn felt bad about it; Ben had been so good to her in the past couple weeks, but it was the only way. She couldn't tell him who she really was.

News had reached Lemeth of the reward her father had offered. A sting of guilt surged through her. She knew her parents were worried about her and, truth be told, she missed them, too. But they wanted to force her into a marriage she could not live with. Once they gave up on finding her, King Edric would appoint a new heir, maybe arrange another marriage, and everyone would be much happier in the long run. Including Emberlynn, who was now free to live her own life for the first time.

The two friends finished their breakfast, packed up their belongings (Emberlynn had none) and headed to the center of Faryn. They pulled up by a line of shops and Ben stopped the cart.

"I need to buy a few provisions for the journey home," he told Emberlynn.

"Mind watching the cart for a quick bit while I run into a shop or two?"

"Not at all."

Ben climbed off the cart, tied his horse's reigns to the hitching post, and crossed the street to the Baker.

Emberlynn hummed to herself as she took in her surroundings. Due to her morning lie in, it was midday already. The city was bustling with people doing ordinary tasks in their ordinary lives. Emberlynn didn't mean that as a putdown; she'd lived most of her life wanting nothing more than to be ordinary. Being a royal had its perks, of course, but it came at a cost. The price had finally become more than she was willing to pay. So this was her future: an ordinary city and an ordinary life. Faryn seemed like as good a place as any to start her new life.

A pair of young women passed the cart, sharing the day's gossip.

"Have you heard? The Ardian princess has been kidnapped!"

"Really? When did it happen?"

"About two weeks ago."

"King Thomas isn't too pleased about losing his niece. Especially after...well...you know."

"*No, I don't know!*" thought Emberlynn. "*Especially after what?*"

She was about to lean down and ask the women what they meant, when she saw a flash of bright blue out of the corner of her eye.

"*Oh no...*"

"Anyway, he's sent his troops out to see if maybe the culprit didn't bring her here to Lemeth."

"*No, no, no...*"

She turned her head and saw a group of armed men in crisp blue uniforms patrolling the street.

"Oh, so that's what they're doing! They're looking for the princess."

"They're kind of cute, don't you think?"

"Well I certainly love a man in uniform."

"Let's call them over here!" the first girl suggested.

"Oooh! We could pretend not to know about the princess... 'What's going on officers? I hope everything's alright.'" She batted her eyelashes.

The girls giggled. Then the first one, presumably the more outgoing of the two, waved to the guards across the street, beckoning them over.

Emberlynn's heart stopped. She had mere seconds to act. She leapt off the cart, flattened herself on the ground, and crawled quickly behind a stack of hay a few feet away. She sat up, peeked around the corner of the pile, and was just about to breathe a sigh of relief when she felt a hand over her mouth, and strong arms pulling her to the ground.

She turned to face her assailant and was stunned to see a handsome boy about her age. He grinned at her and put a finger to his lips.

"Shhhh," he whispered. "I'm not going to hurt you. I just want you to keep quiet."

He removed his hand from her mouth.

She sat up again, brushed herself off, and studied the boy for a moment.

"Next time you want a girl to keep quiet," she whispered back, "try not to make her think you're mugging her."

He gave her a sheepish look and shrugged.

"Sorry."

The pair peeked out from around the hay at the guards. The girls were giggling and touching the medals and sashes on their uniforms while they smiled and exaggerated the various acts of bravery they'd done to receive them.

Emberlynn's leg began to cramp, so she moved it out from under her.

Crack.

To her horror she realized she'd moved her foot onto a rather large twig. One of the guards turned his head in their direction. He slowly took a few steps closer to the pile of hay.

"What are you doing, Carson?" questioned another guard.

"I heard something," he said, matter-of-factly, moving his hand to his sword.

He took another step toward them and Emberlynn flattened herself on the ground, careful to avoid the twig this time. She looked at the boy and found her own panic mirrored in his eyes.

"Oh, give it up, Carson!" his friend said, rolling his eyes. "Stop showing off and get back over here. These lovely ladies have agreed to accompany us to an early lunch."

Carson released his sword and rejoined his group. He looked back in the direction of the noise and shrugged. Then he sauntered off with his companions.

Emberlynn sat there for a moment, still too afraid to move.

"Nice going," said the boy, laughing so she knew he was only teasing. "You almost got us caught."

"Sorry," she said, blushing. "But you did sort of attack me."

"Good point. I didn't mean to scare you."

"I wasn't scared. Just startled."

"Suuuuure."

Emberlynn made a face at him.

"Why were you hiding from the guards, anyway?" Emberlynn asked.

He studied her for a moment and replied, "I could ask the same of you."

The stranger watched the horror creep into her face. After a moment he rustled her hair and added, "We all have our secrets."

Emberlynn smiled at him, looking relieved.

After a moment the boy stood up.

"Now, where have my manners gone?"

He reached a hand down to Emberlynn.

"Name's Jackson," he said, helping her to her feet.

"Hannah. Pleasure to meet you."

The pair stood there for a moment, studying each other.

Jackson was tall and slender, with smooth, sinewy muscles. He had fair skin and jet-black hair. Emberlynn shifted her focus to his face. It, too, was slender and was accented by a small, round nose and large, oval eyes. He wore a boyish grin and a slight flush was creeping its way into his pale cheeks. Then she noticed his eyes. They were bright green, with gold flecks that caught the light when he moved; the sight made her heart skip a beat.

They were quickly approaching the length of time that is acceptable to stare at someone you've just met without speaking, when the silence was broken.

"Hannah!" came Ben's voice from the other side of the hay. "Hannah! Confound it all! Where has that girl run off to?"

Emberlynn turned to her new friend, trying her best to remain calm.

"How would you like to make that whole fake mugging thing up to me?" she asked, quickly, in a hushed tone.

"What did you have in mind?"

"Follow me."

Emberlynn crawled around to the cart and sneaked up behind Ben, with Jackson at her heels.

"Hey, Ben!" said the princess, excitedly, popping up.

"There ye are! Blimey, I was just about to check the stocks," he replied, nudging her arm affectionately.

"The stocks?" asked Jackson, giving her a questioning look.

"Long story..." said Emberlynn, laughing. "Anyway, Ben... I'd like you to meet my cousin, Felix. He walked right past the cart and didn't even see me. He was running some errands in town for my aunt."

"Glad to finally meet you, Felix," said Ben, offering his hand.

"Uh, yeah. You, too, Ben!" he replied, shaking Ben's rather large hand and trying not to look confused. "Thanks for taking such great care of my...cousin."

"T'was a pleasure. She's a fine young lady."

Emberlynn blushed.

"Well, I said I'd deliver her safe to her cousin, and I have. So I guess I'll be on my way back to the Missus."

Emberlynn hadn't really thought about saying goodbye to Ben. She'd always known they'd be parting ways, but she'd never planned on a proper goodbye. Truth be told, it was much harder than she would ever have expected. They'd been traveling together for two weeks. It doesn't seem like a long time when you put it that way, but he had taken care of her and been there for her when she needed help. She knew her parents loved her but, truthfully, Ben felt more like a father to her than King Edric ever had.

As Ben hugged her goodbye a tear betrayed her otherwise together exterior.

"Now, now, Hannah," he said, a bit choked up himself. "Don't sully yer reunion with yer cousin with silly tears. I'll be missin' ye too, young friend. But no goodbye is forever. When ye finish yer stay here in Lemeth, ye know where to find me. Come meet my Sarah. I know she'd be delighted."

"Thanks," said Emberlynn, wiping her eyes and feeling a bit sheepish. "I will. Tell Sarah I'm sorry I kept you. And, Ben. Thank you, truly, for everything."

Ben nodded and climbed aboard his cart.

"Let's head home, shall we, Layla?" he said to his horse. "It's been a long journey here, and we're just getting started."

"I couldn't have said it better myself," thought Emberlynn.

CHAPTER 10

A FORK IN THE ROAD

"So, two questions..." said Jackson, as he watched Ben disappear down the muddy street.

"Go on."

"For starters, what kind of name is Felix?"

Emberlynn laughed.

"I'm serious. Felix is the best you can come up with? Really?"

"Hey, it was the first thing that came to mind, and it's not like I put hours of thought into it."

"I'm just saying. Next time you make up a fake cousin you should give him a cool name like Roan. Or...Ethan, yeah!"

"Would you like me to call you Ethan?" asked Emberlynn with a twinkle in her eye.

"Jackson is fine," he laughed. "But that brings me to my second question: Why am I pretending to be your fake cousin?"

"Well it's a bit of a long story..."she replied, hesitantly.

"That may be. But it sounds exciting. And I can always make time for an exciting story. Where are you headed? I'll walk with you."

"That's a good question. I honestly have no idea."

"Wait. So, you had me help you trick that nice man into leaving you here alone...but you have no idea where you're going?"

"Correct."

"Why, exactly?"

"I can't tell you exactly because I'm not positive myself, but mostly it was because he needed to get back home to his wife. He was just helping me along on my journey to Lemeth. Well, here we are in Lemeth and there didn't seem to be much point in keeping him here while I wandered around trying to figure out what I'm doing. He misses Sarah, I can tell. And I'm sure she's eager to have him home."

"I see. Well...no, really...I don't. Why did you tell him you were coming to visit your cousin if your cousin is just a figment of your imagination?"

"He most certainly is not."

"So you do have a cousin here?"

"Of course. Ben just met him."

Jackson stared at her, unsure what to make of the comment.

"I'm only joking, silly. I do have a cousin in Lemeth. But he doesn't live in Faryn and I'm not here to see him. In fact, I'm hoping to avoid him."

"You two on bad terms or something?"

"Not exactly..."

"Well what, then?"

"It's like you said...we all have our secrets."

"Fair enough," Jackson answered with a laugh. "Well, I can't very well walk you to your destination if you don't have one."

"I was actually hoping you could tell me where I could find an inn with a bath."

"There isn't one in Faryn."

Emberlynn's eyes widened.

"It's such a small town, most people don't travel here. If they do, they only stay a day or two."

"I see. Well, perhaps I should head to the next town over. Maybe it's a little bigger."

"Oh it certainly is. Nice place, Arbourton. They've got two inns there, both with baths in the rooms."

"Well, I guess I should start walking then. Might even be able to make it by sundown. Would you mind terribly pointing me in the right direction?"

"I'd be happy to. But I have a better idea, if you're interested," he interjected

"I'm listening..."

⁓

"This whole Emberlynn situation is really starting to concern me," said Duke Theron to his son, early one evening.

They were sitting around the small drawing room table sharing some early-evening tea.

"Starting?" questioned Banning. "Were you not concerned before now?"

"Not in the same way. We assumed that she had been kidnapped. And maybe she has," he added quickly, in response to a glaring look from his son. "But it's been too long for a kidnapping. A week I could understand, but after King Edric's reward offer...it just doesn't make sense. Kidnappers would either have returned her for the 730 Ryns or sent some sort of ransom note demanding more money."

Theron paused for a moment to take a sip of tea. He set his cup down firmly, wiped his mouth, and continued.

"So, as I see it there are two feasible options: either her captors have no intention of ever releasing her, or..." he trailed off.

"Or...?"

"Emberlynn is starting to remember."

❧

Emberlynn fidgeted nervously as she and Jackson approached the cottage.

"Are you sure this is a good idea?" she asked, smoothing out her hair for the hundredth time.

"Stop fussing," Jackson laughed. "I told you...it's fine. I promise."

"I really can just find an inn."

"Mmhmm, and how much money do you have?"

She stared at him sheepishly.

"That's what I thought. Really, Hannah, my parents will be happy to have you for the night. And my mother knows most of the people in town. She'll be able to tell you if anyone is looking for help in their shop."

"I just hate to impose like this. And on such short notice."

"Mother will draw you a hot bath..." he teased.

"Oh, alright. I can't argue with that."

Jackson's family lived in a simple cottage near the center of Faryn. It was brown stone with ivy climbing merrily up the front. The dark green door blended in with the vines, making it nearly imperceptible. Emberlynn smiled as Jackson opened the door; she was anxious to meet the family she'd heard so much about on the walk over.

"Well, come on then," called Jackson from inside.

She realized she'd been standing outside on the doorstep for at least a minute, staring nervously inside.

"Oh, right," she said awkwardly, as she crossed the threshold.

Jackson closed the door behind her as she stood, wide eyed, taking everything in. Having grown up in a palace, Emberlynn was used to grandeur; truthfully, not much impressed her anymore. But there was something about this little cottage that she absolutely adored. It felt...well, cozy. Everything was placed with great care; books stacked high on shelves, hand embroidered cushions adorning the furniture, sweet little teacups on the table, and simple, but attractive paintings on the walls. The whole place had an almost musty feel, but there wasn't a single speck of dust in sight.

"It's nothing fancy, but we're fond of it," said Jackson, interrupting her thoughts.

"It's perfect," she said.

And she meant it.

"Son, is that you?" called his mother from the other room.

"Hey, Mom," he answered. "Can you come in here for a minute? There's someone I want you to meet."

A slender, petite woman poked her head in from the kitchen. Her long dark hair was braided loosely and pinned messily atop her head.

"Hannah, allow me to present my mother, Charlotte. Mom, this is Hannah."

Charlotte surveyed Emberlynn carefully with deep, wise eyes and slightly pursed lips. After a few seconds she smiled warmly.

"It's a pleasure to meet you, Hannah."

Emberlynn smiled back and started to speak, when Jackson cut her off.

"Hannah has journeyed all the way from Ardia and just parted ways with her traveling companion. She was asking directions to the inn, though I'm not sure why," he said, shooting the princess a good-natured smile. "She was mugged outside of Laith and lost all her money and belongings. And I scared her half to death when I met her, as well. Goodness, you've had quite the adventure, haven't you?" he added, turning to Emberlynn again.

"You poor dear!" Charlotte exclaimed.

"I offered her our spare room for the night," Jackson continued. "And I thought you might know someone in the village who could use some help in their shop."

"As a matter of fact, I do...but first," she said, turning to Emberlynn, "I think this one is in need of a hot bath."

CHAPTER 11

FLASHBACKS AND FAIRY DUST

Jackson and his family sat around the dinner table eating a vegetable stew that Charlotte had made.

"This is delicious, Dear, as always," said Jackson's father.

"Thank you, Cavan," she said, giving him a quick kiss on the cheek.

Emberlynn loved Jackson's family from the moment she met them. Cavan was a tall slender man with dark hair and bright green eyes, like his son. They had surprisingly muscular frames from their work on the farm but, despite their time in the sun, both had smooth, pale skin.

"He's very educated for a farmer," noted Emberlynn.

Indeed, Cavan spoke with knowledge and authority and, when he spoke, you couldn't help but listen. Emberlynn's eyes wandered to the bookshelves lining one entire wall of the house. They were filled with maps, books of history and art, and many others Emberlynn had never seen.

"I'm sorry, what was that?" she asked, suddenly realizing that Cavan had been talking to her. "I'm afraid I'm a bit tired from my journey."

"Of course you are," he said, kindly. "That small frame was not built for long travels. But I'd only just begun speaking. It's no trouble to repeat myself. I was saying that business has really been taking off for my Charlotte in the shop—people bringing their clothes to be mended or wanting new party dresses and such. It's great for us, but there's only so much she and Kinleigh can do at one time. They've found themselves falling a bit behind in the past few weeks."

Emberlynn nodded.

"How are you at sewing, young lady?" Charlotte asked her.

"Not very good, I'm afraid. That is, I've never exactly tried it before," she answered, sheepishly.

"Not to worry. Do you think you could take orders and write down measurements if I showed you how?"

"Oh, I'm sure I could!"

"Well then, if you're interested we can try you out as an apprentice in my shop."

"Mother is the best seamstress within a hundred miles," said Jackson, grinning.

"Don't exaggerate, dear," she said laughing.

"I'm not!" he turned to Emberlynn. "I'm not. She's just being modest."

"Anyway," Charlotte continued, with a smile, "I'm afraid we couldn't pay you much. There's only about 5 Gossle a week in the budget. But Cavan and I have agreed that we can offer you our spare room while you're with us."

It was more than she could ever have asked or expected. She was at a loss for words; overcome with gratitude. After a moment she managed to speak.

"Such acts of kindness to a complete stranger..." said Emberlynn, slowly. "It's unlike anything I've ever known."

She smiled, thinking of Ben.

"Until this journey I had never met anyone so willing to help another soul in need. It's truly inspiring."

She sat there for a moment, and let it all sink in. Then she added, "I will do my very best to earn your respect and to repay your kindness in any way I can."

Jackson's sister, Kinleigh, had sat through the majority of the meal in silence. She had long dark hair, like her mother, and her deep red lips were pursed as she listened intently to the conversation going on around her. She was only fifteen, but she carried herself with the quiet strength of one who has seen much of life. It was not that she was an ungracious host; rather she was quite shy. In her experience one never knew whom to trust, so it was better to start out cautious. Kinleigh had spent these moments of silence trying to decide how she felt about this strange girl sitting across the table from her, but Emberlynn's speech showed her to be as sincere and genuine as anyone could be. Having made up her mind, Kinleigh finally joined the conversation.

"It will be a pleasure working with you," she said. "Mother and I can begin your training in the morning."

✍

Banning rose quickly from the table, a look of concern on his face.

"What does this mean for us?" he asked, nervously.

"As for the future, I cannot tell. But for the present..."

Theron stood also and took a deep breath.

"Marshall!" he called.

"What is it, sir?" Marshall asked, walking swiftly into the room.

"Please prepare the carriage immediately. Banning and I must pay a visit to the King to say our goodbyes. In light of the current situation we feel it best we return to Lemeth. We can no longer, in good conscience, impose upon His Highness' hospitality. And we hope to be of some service to King Thomas in the search for the princess back home, as she really could be anywhere at this point."

Marshall bowed and went to get the carriage ready for the journey to the palace. When he returned, he found the Duke and his son had already begun packing.

"The carriage is ready, Your Grace."

"Thank you for preparing it so quickly," said the Duke, smiling at Marshall. "We shouldn't be long, and when we return I would greatly appreciate your help in loading up our things. We plan to leave for Lemeth at first light."

"Yes, Your Grace."

Marshall helped them into the carriage then returned inside. He noted several boxes and bags already stacked by the door.

"*Those two don't waste any time,*" he thought, as he crossed the room.

As Marshall passed the baggage, he tripped over a small box that was sticking out from the stack.

"*Oof!*"

The box flew open, spilling a pile of odd trinkets onto the floor. Marshall hastily gathered them up, placing them carefully back in the box.

"Nothing seems to have broken," he noted, with a sigh of relief.

He latched the box and placed it back in the pile. Then he started to stand.

Clink.

His foot knocked into a small glass bottle, which he picked up and studied carefully. At first it seemed like nothing more than a vile of dirt. But as he moved it, it began to swirl upward in the bottle, catching the light. He shook it and held it up in the direction of the window.

It was the most beautiful thing he had ever seen. It seemed as if someone had bottled the stars on a cloudless night; the strange substance danced and winked at him from within its glass prison. Marshall didn't know what this was, but he had a feeling it was something the Duke did not want him to see. He was just about to return it to its box when he heard the sound of hooves in the drive. How could they be back already? He must have stared into the bottle for longer than he realized.

The door swung open and Marshall had only seconds to act. He stood swiftly, shoved the bottle into his pocket, took a few steps across the foyer, and turned to face the door.

"Your Grace!" he said with a smile, walking toward him. "Nice to see you back so soon. I was wondering if you would like me to call for dinner before or after you do your packing?"

"Now would be wonderful," was the reply. "We shall continue our packing as the staff prepares the meal, and when it is ready we shall stop and have some."

"I'll do that right away then, sir."

Marshall walked away as quickly as he could without looking suspicious. His heart was pounding as he closed the kitchen door, breathing a sigh of relief.

"That was close."

The Duke turned to his son and said, "That strange servant seems to have finally warmed up to us, just in time for our departure."

Banning shrugged, and the pair went off to pack the rest of their belongings.

"Georgia!" Marshall whispered, as he crossed the kitchen. "Yes?"

"I need to ask you something."

"Sure. What's up?"

He motioned for her to follow him. They went into the small servant's hallway in back of the kitchen, and Marshall looked quickly around to make sure no one else was around. Then he pulled the little bottle out of his pocket.

Georgia gasped.

"Where did you get that?" she asked seriously, a mix of fear and curiosity in her eyes.

"That's sort of a long story," he said, with a wave of his hand. "I was hoping you could tell me what this is," he continued, holding the vial up for her to examine more closely.

"That is fairy dust."

"Fairy dust?!"

Georgia nodded.

They heard a creak and glanced at the door with bated breath. When no one entered, Marshall continued.

"And where exactly would someone get something like this?"

"Well, unless you steal it," Georgia answered, giving him a stern look, "There are only two ways to get a vial of fairy dust."

⌘

"I'll never forget you!"

The words rang out like ripples through the fog. Emberlynn watched the shadow of their owner disappear into the trees, and was gripped with fear. She didn't stop to think, she just ran, as fast as her legs could carry her.

"Your Highness!" came a different voice from right in front of her. "Emberlynn, where are you?"

She turned and fled the voice—sprinting in the other direction until her pale pink dress snagged on a root, bringing her crashing to the ground.

Ahh!

The princess cried out in pain as she fell, but she knew there was no time to waste. She pulled herself to her feet and limped onward until...

Thud!

She collided with someone in the darkness and felt a pair of arms squeezing her a little too tightly.

"There you are, Princess! We've been looking everywhere."

She struggled against her captor, but it was no use.

"Calm down, Princess. This will all be over in just a moment."

An icy breeze blew through the forest. Emberlynn's whole body shook violently as the cold overtook her.

Emberlynn sat up with a start, breathing heavily.

"Where...?" she mumbled sleepily.

She blinked a few times, taking in her surroundings as she slowly remembered the day before. She snuggled down into the blankets in her very own bed in a tiny room in a precious little cottage on the very edge of Lemeth.

"*Safe,*" she thought, with a sigh of contentment. "*Safe, free, and about to start the first day of a brand new life that's all my own.*"

Emberlynn climbed out of bed and surveyed herself in the small round mirror hanging above the dresser in the corner of her room. She looked a little haggard, worn from her long journey here, but she was well rested, clean, and had been given a fresh nightgown.

"*There's no limit to the difference a hot bath and set of clean clothes can make,*" she thought, smiling.

She ran her fingers through her hair, carefully removing any tangles from her gentle waves. Then she took a deep breath and opened the door.

"Good morning, Hannah!" called Charlotte cheerfully, looking up from the stove. "Breakfast should be ready in a bit."

"Good morning. It smells wonderful!," Emberlynn replied.

"I trust you slept well?"

"Very well, thank you."

"Morning, Hannah!" Jackson called from the table. "I made tea, if you'd like some."

He gestured to the empty seat across from him.

"I'd love some."

Emberlynn sat down and poured herself a hot cup of strong tea.

"Mmm," she sighed, taking the first sip from her cup. "It's been weeks since I had a good cup of tea."

Emberlynn had never experienced a real family breakfast before. She usually ate with her parents, but her father was always poring over stacks of paper—laws, letters, and other kingly business. Her mother spent most mornings confirming her appointments with the royal tailor, chef, decorator, etc. They exchanged pleasantries, but rarely engaged in meaningful conversation.

It was nice to see family taking an interest in each other's lives for a change. She supposed most families probably spent quality time together. But she wasn't from "most families."

Charlotte placed breakfast on the table and sat down to join her family.

"Eat up," Kinleigh advised, smiling. "We've got a lot of work to do."

After breakfast Kinleigh tossed Emberlynn a bundle of clothes.

"It's a spare set of mine," she explained.

Emberlynn caught them and tucked them under her arm. "Thanks."

"They may be a bit small," continued Kinleigh, who had her mother's figure. "But it should work for today, until we can get your measurements and make you some of your own."

After Emberlynn had changed, Charlotte and Kinleigh took her into town to their seamstress shop. It reminded her of their cottage in many ways: it was small, quaint, and welcoming. The whole shop was piled high with bolts of fabric, boxes of needles, rolls of thread, and other things Emberlynn couldn't identify. There was a workbench against the far wall covered in stacks of papers and garments that were being made or mended. She took everything in with wide eyes.

"It's a bit overwhelming at," admitted Kinleigh, laughing, "Which is why we could use the help."

"Why don't we get started on your measurements?" Charlotte suggested. "That way we can show you how it's done, since that's what you'll be doing to start. And then we can make you something that will fit a little better."

"I'm afraid it will take me quite a long time to pay you for the clothes."

"Don't be silly, dear," responded Charlotte. "We'll simply use scraps left from other pieces we have made. And as for labor, it will be a good introduction for you to what tailoring is all about. It sounds all very even."

Emberlynn smiled warmly at the older woman's generosity.

Charlotte had Emberlynn stand on a small platform while she wrapped a string with markings on it around various parts of her body. She scribbled down numbers on a piece of paper as she went.

"These marks on the string tell you what size the garment needs to be," she explained. "See this was the measurement for your waist. So you write it down here…"

They had Emberlynn practice on Kinleigh, and after a few tries she managed to get her correct measurements.

"Well done, Hannah. Okay, it's about time to open the shop. Kinleigh, can you find Mrs. Millins' dress in the pile over there?" Charlotte asked, pointing to a chair in the corner.

"She'll be here to pick it up this morning. And Hannah, can you open that bottom drawer in that cabinet and find the stack of fresh papers for today's orders?"

As she finished saying this an elderly man came into the shop carrying a jacket with a rather large tear in the sleeve. From that point on there were patrons coming in and out of the shop until sundown. They took a short break for lunch, although Charlotte spent most of it working on a shirt for Emberlynn. Then it was back to work. Emberlynn enjoyed it, though, and by the end of the day she was taking measurements all by herself.

The next morning Charlotte taught Emberlynn how to take orders for new garments. In addition to taking measurements, she was to find out the occasion for which it was being ordered as well as what color and type of fabric the customer wanted. She spent the next few days familiarizing herself with the selection of fabric in the shop.

Before she knew it, a month had gone by. Charlotte had made her a few sets of clothes so she didn't have to wear Kinleigh's anymore. Emberlynn had grown close to Jackson's family and was beginning to feel at home in Faryn. She was pleasantly surprised to find that she was good at her job. She learned the inventory quickly and was now making suggestions to the patrons about fabric and design choices for their orders. If there was one thing she had gained from her years of being dressed up and paraded around at the palace, it was an eye for fashion.

Emberlynn was enjoying her new life as a commoner but, truth be told, she hadn't expected it to be so much work. The shop was closed a day or two every week, but that didn't mean she had time off. Charlotte used those days to teach her how to mend and sew, order new fabrics from other villages, and do other little things that would be useful around the shop.

Emberlynn awoke one morning to the sound of birds singing outside. She rolled out of bed and walked over to her window. The sun was streaming in and she sighed as she melted into its warmth. Summer had come to Lemeth.

"Good morning," Emberlynn called cheerily, as she walked into the kitchen. "It's such a lovely day!"

"Indeed it is," said Cavan. "It's a shame, you and Kinleigh being cooped up inside on a day like this."

"It's a shame to be stuck doing anything, really," added Jackson, who was scheduled to work on the farm that day with his father.

"Well, the shop is closed today," said Charlotte. "And you girls have been working so hard. Why don't you take the day off?"

"We can go swimming at the lake!" Kinleigh beamed.

"No fair!" cried Jackson. "You can't go swimming without me," he stated, matter-of-factly.

"Oh, go on, then," said Cavan, laughing. "I can handle the farm today. Maybe I'll even make it a short day and have some sport myself. A little hunting, perhaps."

With that settled, they hastily ate their breakfasts and headed down to the small lake on the edge of the village. Jackson and Kinleigh didn't waste any time. As soon as the lake was in sight, they ran to it and jumped right it. Jackson made a giant splash and came up laughing.

Emberlynn stood on the edge of the water, squishing her toes in the mud. She closed her eyes as the breeze gently blew her hair. And suddenly she was thirteen. The sun was shining in a clear blue sky as she stood on the beach looking out at the ocean. Everything was a little hazy, but she could make out a group of boys chasing each other around and splashing in the water.

One of them called to her, "Come on, Emmie! The water's great!"

She felt her heart warm as he said her name, and took off running toward him. She was almost to the water when she heard a stern voice from behind her.

"Emberlynn, come here."

She turned and walked slowly back across the beach.

"Yes, Father?"

"What were you doing?"

"I was just going to play in the water."

"Emberlynn, princesses don't splash around in the water."

"Well then what do princesses do?"

"Act like ladies."

"Are you coming?" came the voice from the water.

She stood there, cemented in place by her father's wishes.

"Hey! Are you coming? Hannah?!"

Emberlynn's eyes flew open with a start.

Jackson and Kinleigh were looking up at her questioningly.

"Sorry, I guess I was daydreaming."

"Well, come on then. The water's great!"

She took a deep breath.

"Princesses make their own destinies, father," she said, quietly.

And with that, Hannah dived headfirst into the lake.

CHAPTER 12

MAGIC AND MYTH

Banning and his father arrived at the Lemethian palace, in the city of Gillodel, on a warm afternoon in June. King Thomas greeted them as they climbed out of their carriage.

"Theron," said the king, gripping his hand, "Do you bring any word of my niece?"

"I'm afraid not, Your Majesty," the Duke replied, somberly.

Thomas' face fell. It had been two months since Emberlynn's disappearance and hope was fading fast.

"Well, do come inside. I'm sure you are tired from your journey. I'll call for tea and we can discuss this dreadful situation. Maybe you or Banning will have some ideas on how we can improve our search. Prince Damian will join us when he returns from his afternoon ride."

"You two go ahead," said Banning. "I'd like to stretch my legs for a moment. I'll be there shortly."

Banning walked around to the back of the palace and cautiously opened the garden gate. He slowly walked through it and began pacing around the gardens.

"This is where it all started," he thought. *"This has been years in the making. I'm so close and I'm not going to lose it all now..."*

A look of determination overtook the handsome face as he shut the gate firmly behind him. Warily, he stole one last backward glance before heading returning to the front of the palace and joining his father and the king.

"I must find her..."

⁓

The sun had set by the time Hannah, Jackson, and Kinleigh returned home. They had packed a picnic lunch to eat by the lake, splashed around for a few hours, then climbed up the hill to the Ardian-Lemethian border. Their plan was to watch the sunset over Faryn. That was when the day got truly interesting.

They had just reached the top of the hill when they saw a flash of dark green; a small group of Ardian cavalrymen was riding toward them. Hannah's heart stopped in her chest. She thought about running but didn't want to raise suspicion. Instead she took a deep breath and stood her ground.

"Good evening," called one of the cavalrymen, as they approached.

"Evening," Jackson called back, stepping protectively in front of the girls. "What brings you lads to Lemeth?"

"We've business with the King. His Majesty King Edric sent us."

"I see."

"And what are you three doing hanging around the Ardian border so late?" asked the cavalryman, giving them a suspicious look.

"Watching the sunset," Jackson replied, matter-of-factly.

Suddenly, the man's brow furrowed and he looked intently past Jackson at the girls. He climbed swiftly off his horse and approached them.

100

"Everything ok?" Jackson asked, his hand slowly forming a fist at his side.

The man ignored him and circled around to Hannah, surveying her slowly.

"Can I help you?" she asked sternly, trying to keep her voice level.

"Have we met before?"

"No, I don't believe so."

"You sure? You remind me of someone I know. But I can't quite place it."

"Well, have you been to Lemeth before? Because I've never been to Ardia."

"No..." he answered slowly.

"In that case I am quite sure we have never met," replied Hannah firmly.

"Right...um, carry on then," said the man, finally, climbing back on his horse. "Let's go, men."

With that the company rode on, leaving the three alone atop the hill.

Hannah sat down and pulled her knees to her chest. She took in a deep breath as she looked down at the sun setting over Faryn. Then she exhaled slowly. Kinleigh sat down beside her and gave her a questioning look. She was about to offer up a lame excuse about having "one of those faces," when Jackson plopped down on her other side and burst out laughing.

"What's so funny?" asked the girls, in unison. This made them giggle.

"But seriously..." Hannah continued, regaining her composure, "Why are you laughing?"

He paused for a moment. "We all have our secrets," he responded finally, with an impish grin.

Hannah chuckled.

"Did I miss something?" Kinleigh questioned.

Jackson ignored her and turned to Hannah. We should probably head back now. It will be dark soon. He stood and helped Hannah to her feet.

"What?" called Kinleigh, as the pair headed down the hill, "What did I miss?"

She shot up, grabbed the picnic basket, and headed after them.

"Wait up, you two!"

When they returned home, dinner was waiting for them.

"How was your day?" asked Charlotte.

"Interesting..." was Jackson's reply.

"How so?" questioned Cavan.

"Oh, I just meant...it was a lot of fun."

Then Kinleigh chimed in.

"No, what he meant was—*oof!*"

Jackson stomped on her foot under the table and shot her a stern look out of the corner of his eye. She stared at him for a second before continuing...

"What he meant was, uh, he...well we had a race. And he lost. So...he has to help with dishes today instead of me."

She smiled in response to Jackson's glare.

"Uh, yeah. That's what I meant..."

Hannah hadn't spoken during the meal and was staring blankly into what was left of her stew.

"Hannah, are you alright, dear?" asked Charlotte. "Hannah?"

"Oh!" she said, looking up with a start. "Oh, uh, yeah. Sorry. I'm just...tired, I guess. Long day."

"I'm sure it was, keeping my two in check all day," Charlotte replied, laughing.

Hannah let out a giggle, which quickly turned into a yawn.

"Why don't you get some rest, dear? You look positively spent."

"I think I will turn in for the night. Thank you for the lovely dinner."

She headed back to her room, shut the door, and sat down upon her bed. Picking up the small hand mirror from her bedside table, she studied her face intently in its reflection.

She saw the same face she'd seen for eighteen years— the same deep blue eyes, her father's nose, her mother's chin... the face of Emberlynn, Princess of Ardia...but it was different somehow. The eyes held a wisdom and a fire that made her look older. The royal porcelain skin had bronzed and was beginning to freckle...the face of Hannah, assistant in the seamstress shop of Faryn. She was both of those people, and both of those people were her. But she couldn't be two people at once; she couldn't be royal and free.

She pulled the signet ring out from beneath her shirt and turned it over in her hand. Then she unclasped the chain and slipped the ring off, leaving only the key around her neck. Opening the drawer of her bedside table, she placed the ring gently at the back of it. Then she pulled out the pair of scissors lying beside it. Her hair had grown quite a bit in the past few months and she couldn't have anything giving her away. It was much too close a call with the cavalryman up on the hill. She took the scissors and slowly cut her hair again until it fell just below her chin. She put the scissors back in the drawer, along with the pieces of hair she had cut, placing them in front of her ring. Then she covered both objects with a small book on sewing Charlotte had lent her. She picked up the mirror again and smiled at the face staring back at her: Hannah of Faryn.

Hannah changed into her nightgown, splashed some water on her face, and slipped under the covers. She blew out her candle and was just curling up in bed when she heard the sound of whispers coming from somewhere nearby. Kinleigh's room lay on the other side of the wall by Hannah's head. She and Jackson were arguing, trying to keep their voices down.

"Why didn't you want Mother and Father to know about the cavalrymen?" demanded Kinleigh.

"Because I didn't want to worry them."

"You don't think they—"

"No," Jackson cut her off. "No I'm sure they don't."

"Well, why then?"

Hannah scooted to the top of her bed and listened.

"It had nothing to do with us. They carried a message for the king. I'm sure it was regarding the princess."

"Emberlynn? Do you think they've found her? I've been so worried!"

"No. They haven't found her."

On the other side of the wall Hannah's eyes widened.

"How do you know?"

Hannah leaned in closer and pressed her ear to the wall. The bed let out a small creak.

"What was that?" asked Jackson.

"I'm sure it was nothing. Jackson, tell me what you know."

He paused for a moment, thinking.

"Later..." he said. "Get some sleep, Kins."

Hannah heard footsteps as Jackson crossed the room. He lingered in the doorway for a moment before adding, "I know you don't remember that night like I do. You weren't yet ten."

"You mean the night Aedyn—"

"Yes. Kinleigh, that night changed everything. And I think they're about to change again. Just...be careful."

More footsteps, the sound of two closing doors, and the pounding of Hannah's heart in her chest.

Aedyn.

That name stirred something in Hannah. Why did that name sound so familiar? What night was Jackson referring to? And why didn't he want anyone to hear them talking about it?

These questions circled around in her head as she drifted off into a deep sleep.

"Emberlynn..." came a voice from the darkness. "Emberlynn!"

Her eyes shot open, and there she was in the marble room staring at the silver door.

Knock knock knock.

"Emberlynn!" came the voice again, from beyond the door.

"Y-y-yes...?" she asked slowly, her voice shaking.

"Emberlynn. Do you remember?"

"Remember? Remember what?"

"Do you remember what happened that night?"

"What night?"

"That night? Do you remember?"

Knock knock.

"I don't—I don't know. I don't know what you're talking about!" she cried desperately.

"Remember!" demanded the voice, again.

It was a man's voice—deep, smooth, and familiar.

"You must remember!"

"I don't!" she yelled back, tears streaming from her eyes. "I can't!"

Her head began to ache.

Knock knock knock.

She ran to the door and grabbed hold of the handle, trying desperately to force it open.

"You must remember!"

She banged her fists on the door as hard as she could.

"I can't!"

Bang.

"I don't remember!"

Bang.

"I—*aahhhhggh!*"

Her hand slipped, catching on the intricate designs and slicing open. Blood dripped slowly down her arm and onto the door. The door began to glow again, bits of fairy dust churning up where drops of her blood had splattered. Then slowly the dust began to dart about, being pulled toward the handle like a black hole. It was forming something. A pattern...a picture...? A keyhole.

"Remember!" came the voice, startling Hannah.

"I—"

She pulled the key out from under her shirt. She felt like she was underwater; everything was moving in slow motion. Leaning in she lifted the key and moved it toward the lock. Suddenly she sneezed violently, jolting herself awake.

"No!" she cried, as she sat up in bed.

Hannah shut her eyes, trying to force herself back asleep—back into that room.

"Remember..." rang the voice inside her head.

"I can't..." she whispered.

Hannah looked down to see the key resting in the palm of her hand in a pool of her own blood. She rinsed it off in the basin of water on her dresser and bandaged it. The sun was just rising over the trees as she dressed, tucking the key safely beneath her clothes.

Jackson and his family were still asleep when Hannah tiptoed silently into the kitchen. She scarfed down a chunk of bread and some meat, then sneaked quietly out of the cottage.

She passed a few people in town but, for the most part, the streets were deserted. Most shops wouldn't be opening for at least another hour but Tilford, the man who ran the bookshop, was an early riser and known to open his shop with the sunrise. When Hannah arrived, she looked over her shoulder to make sure no one was watching. She wasn't sure why, but she didn't think she wanted anyone to see her there. Reassured that the coast was clear she pushed gently on the door and it swung open with a soft cling of the bell.

"Morning, Hannah!" called Tilford, cheerily. "You're out and about rather early this morning."

Tilford was in his mid-thirties. He had dark curls, bright eyes, and a kind smile. His family had run the bookshop in Faryn for generations; he knew each and every book and where to find it.

"I am," she replied. "Cavan's birthday is coming up and, well they've been so kind to me. I wanted to get him something—a book maybe?"

"A splendid idea. Did you have something in mind?"

"Not precisely. But I thought I might browse the history section."

"Ah history. Those are in the back corner, behind that row of shelves there."

"Thank you. Oh, and I was hoping maybe you wouldn't mention this to anyone, it being a surprise and all."

"Of course."

Hannah walked to the back corner of the shop and found a small shelf lined with thick books on the history of the three great kingdoms of the realm: Ardia, Lemeth, and Tardyn. She had never been to Tardyn before, but she knew a fair amount about if from her studies. It lay northwest of Ardia, over the Banwen Mountains, and beyond the Enalei Desert. They allied with Ardia and Lemeth in the Great War, a century ago. The palace, in the capital city of Gelmyrh, was said to be carved out of a sheer cliff face of deep black rock, overlooking the Denberlaé Sea.

"*But this is not why I'm here,*" thought Hannah, turning her focus back to the row of books.

"*Let's see...'Ancient Lemeth,' 'The Great War,' no...*"

She ran her fingers over the books as she read the titles.

"*No, no, no...Hmmm, 'Chronicles of the Kingdoms,' let's try that...*"

She pulled it from the shelf, cracked it open, and stopped on a random page.

"*Section Four: Ardian Nobility.*"

As she turned the pages, Hannah saw the faces of her ancestors; Queen Adelaide, who had a line of royal horses bred, King Jonathan, who banished the dragons from Ardia...she flipped the page again and smiled at the face staring back at her.

"*Queen Cinderella,*" she thought. "*People always told me I have her eyes. But she reigned centuries ago...*"

The princess flipped through the entire book, finding nothing of use. She was about to place it back on the shelf when she realized something.

"*There's a page missing.*"

The last page of the book had been carelessly ripped out, leaving jagged pieces behind. Hannah had a funny feeling that this page had something to do with...whatever it was she was trying to figure out. She sighed as she placed the book back on the shelf. She was just about to leave when something caught her eye.

At the very back of the shelf, lying behind a volume on the history and changes of Lemethian architecture, was a small book of deep red leather. As Hannah looked closer the letters on the spine started to glow. She picked it up and studied it intently.

" '*Magic and Myth.' What are you?*" she whispered.

Hannah opened the book and immediately sneezed, a shower of dust erupting from the pages. She had always loved the smell of old books, but this was the downside of that. Hannah sneezed again, then turned her attention back to the book. She waited for the dust to settle then gently flipped the page, pausing when she reached a section on fairies.

Fairy dust is a mysterious substance with magic properties.
Not much is known about it, as it is very rare.
There are only two ways to obtain fairy dust:
One must either
   1. Save a fairy's life, receiving some as a gift, or
   2. Kill a fairy, taking some by force

Hannah shuddered, and turned the page again.
"Magical Properties of Water? No thank you."
Flip.
"Myths About Toads. How many myths about toads are there?"
There were nine.
Flip. Flip.
"Magical Families: Fact or Fiction?"

There is some debate among scholars as to whether "magical families" exist.
Some argue that magical ability could be passed down from one generation to another.
Others insist that the magic is external, tied to the event or giver (i.e. fairy godmothers.)
Either way, most people agree the age of 'the magics' died with the Age of the Fairies.

It is theoretically possible that some magic could be passed down to one's children, even if it is not expressed in the individual. Some magic, fairy magic, for example, leaves very little trace; however more powerful magic could conceivably be more permanent.
The most powerful known magic is that of true love's kiss.

Hannah rolled her eyes.

"Interesting, but cheesy."

Hannah heard footsteps behind her and hastily closed the book, placing it back on the shelf. She had a feeling she wasn't supposed to be looking at this particular book.

"Did you find something for Cavan?" inquired the bookkeeper.

"I was thinking about this book on architecture," she said, holding up the surprisingly large manuscript in her hand. She hadn't had time to put it back on the shelf.

"Excellent choice," he said. "I'm sure Cavan will enjoy it."

Hannah smiled and nodded. Cavan actually did have a birthday in a few weeks. While that wasn't the reason for her visit to the shop, she figured she would get it for him anyway. He probably would enjoy it, being such a lover of the written word. Unfortunately she hadn't had much luck on her real search.

"I do wonder what was on that missing page," she thought, wistfully.

"Oh goodness!" she exclaimed, when they had made their way to the front of the shop. "The sun is already all the way up! How long have I been here?"

"Just shy of an hour."

"Oh my. I'm going to be late for work!" she exclaimed, smacking herself in the forehead.

"Don't worry, Hannah," Tilford assured her, as she paid for the book. "You're only a little late, and I'm sure they won't mind terribly. Tell Charlotte, at least, about your errand. She won't hold it against you."

"Thank you!" Hannah called, grabbing the book and heading quickly out the door.

CHAPTER 13

THE OTHER SIDE

Queen Gwyneria was sitting on her daughter's bed, the fairy necklace in her hands, when her husband found her.

"There you are, my dear," he said, relief evident in his voice. "I've been searching for you all morning."

She stared at the necklace for a few more moments before looking up at him.

"Where is she, Edric?" she asked. Her voice sounded hollow and lifeless. "It's been more than three months since she disappeared."

"I wish I knew," he replied, sitting down beside her and taking her hand. "I sent a few members of the guard with a message to your brother. I've doubled the reward for her safe return. Hopefully..." he trailed off.

He wasn't sure what he hoped for. His daughter had been gone for such a long time that hope had nearly forsaken him. His daughter, and only remaining heir...

"Come now, Gwyn," the king said gently, as tears began to fall down his wife's face, "We mustn't give up. We'll find her. I'm sure of it."

He wasn't. But he needed to be. He needed to believe it.

Gwyneria leaned her head on her husband's shoulder and cried.

"*We mustn't give up,*" he repeated, in his head. "*We mustn't give up...*"

⁓

Theron and Banning had been back home in Gillodel for two weeks and not much had been accomplished. They had hoped Emberlynn would turn up by now, but there was no sign of her.

Banning was pacing around the front hall of Whitehawk Estate when Prince Damian entered.

"Your Highness," he said, bowing. "How can I help you?"

"My parents and I have been planning a grand ball for my upcoming birthday for quite some time—long before my cousin...disappeared," said the prince, stumbling awkwardly over the last word. "We were certain she would have turned up by now. That is, we continued our plans in full confidence that she would be back in time for the celebration. Things being as they are...well, my father feels like it would be best to proceed with the ball as planned. It would be good for the kingdom to have some sort of...distraction...from this dreadful mess. She isn't our princess, but we feel her loss heavily. I do particularly, her being my cousin. We were always very close. Up until..." He trailed off.

"Up until that dreadful night five years ago..." Banning finished.

"She hasn't been quite the same since," Damian replied, pain evident in his eyes. "And now..." He shrugged. "At any rate...my father feels it would be best to—"

"Proceed with the ball as planned?"

"Right, I suppose I said that already. We wanted to make sure you were okay with that. She is your betrothed, after all. I can understand it you would prefer—"

"Of course you must have the ball," Banning interjected. "I think we could all use some sort of distraction."

Damian nodded.

"I'll go tell my father, then. We'll send out the herald at once."

He patted Banning on the back before taking his leave.

"Oh, that dreadful night five years ago..." said Theron, mockingly, as he entered from the adjacent room.

Banning rolled his eyes at his father.

"What did you want me to say, Father? That night that everything went according to plan?"

"Well, almost everything," Theron retorted. "Emberlynn has a nasty habit of being in the wrong place at the wrong time. But I suppose everything worked out in the end."

"Aren't you forgetting something? The small issue of the princess disappearing?"

"Ah, but you're operating under the assumption that we need her."

"Well, don't we?"

"Not necessarily."

Banning gave his father a questioning look.

"Oh, ideally she'll turn up from here or there...or wherever she's been off to."

Theron flicked his hand as if absentmindedly swatting at a fly.

"But if she doesn't, I think we can still work things out for our benefit."

"And how do you propose we do that?"

"Let me worry about that. For now, let's just enjoy the upcoming ball. Then we can take care of this minor detail by paying a little visit to King Edric."

"Very well. But Father...?"

"Hmm?"

"What if she has remembered?"

"My boy, if she had remembered I don't think she'd still be sitting back doing nothing. No I think it's safe to say that she has not—at least not fully."

"And what if she does remember? Fully, I mean."

"We will cross that bridge when we come to it. If we come to it. But for now..."

"The ball?"

"The ball."

Theron turned and left the way he had come, leaving Banning alone once again, pacing back and forth in the front hall of Whitehawk.

The ball for Damian's birthday was set for the third week of August and the whole kingdom was invited. This caused quite a commotion as everyone scurried to get ready for the festivities. Charlotte was known as the best seamstress in twenty miles, so ladies from the surrounding villages came pouring in hoping to have her make their dresses. This meant piles of work for Kinleigh and Hannah as well. Hannah took all the orders and measurements, cut the fabric, and tracked the progress of each dress. Charlotte and Kinleigh spent most of their time bent over the workbench in the shop, sewing, stitching, hemming... Often they worked late into the evening, long past sundown.

One such evening the girls came home to a table set with three plates of cold ham and potatoes; the boys had long since gone to bed. They scarfed down their suppers and Charlotte told the girls to go to bed while she scrubbed up the last of the dishes.

"Why don't you let me take care of that?" asked Hannah. "You've had a much busier day than I have. Besides, there aren't that many and I'm not that tired. Honestly."

Charlotte hugged Hannah tiredly, then shuffled off to her room.

Hannah cleared the table and scrubbed the plates. Then she picked up the candle and was about to head to her own bed when she had a sudden change of heart.

"It's such a beautiful night..."

She grabbed a scarf from the hook by the door and headed outside. Walking around the side of the house, she made her way to the big oak tree and climbed up. Then she scurried out onto a large branch that stretched toward the house. When she reached the end, she swung herself, very carefully, onto the roof, landing with a gentle *thump*.

Crawling to the center of the roof, Hannah lay back and stared up at the sky full of stars. The beautiful thing about stars was they were the same no matter where she went; she was miles and miles from home, but still she saw the same familiar constellations that she'd seen all her life from the window of her bedroom. She stretched out her finger and traced the lines of her favorite one; Adelaide—a picture of a stallion, named for the Ardian queen who had bred the royal line of horses. She thought of Artemis and smiled.

Hannah heard a soft *thump* beside her and sat up with a start.

"Sorry to scare you," whispered Jackson, landing on the roof beside her.

"You like doing that, don't you?" she asked, smiling.

He laughed quietly and sat down beside her.

"I thought you were asleep," she continued.

"Nah, just lying awake, thinking."

"About what?"

"Nothing...and everything."

He sighed, lying down and placing his hands behind his head.

"Things are crazy right now, huh?" he said, though it wasn't really a question.

"This ball has put the whole kingdom in a tizzy," said Hannah, settling back down beside him.

"Yeah, it has. But that's not really what I meant."

Hannah turned her head and looked at Jackson questioningly. He didn't answer, but turned as well, looking intently into her eyes. It reminded her of the day they met, hiding behind the pile of hay by the market. Staring into those eyes Hannah saw the stars...and the sea...and a hundred sunrises.

Jackson reached out slowly and put his hand on top of hers. She froze for a moment, forgetting how to breathe. She and Jackson had grown close over the past few months. He made her laugh, and being with him felt like the most natural thing in the world—like breathing. She studied the curves of his face in the starlight. She couldn't deny he was handsome. And charming. But...

Hannah heard a familiar echo in the back of her mind.

"I'll never forget you!"

She shot up suddenly, trying to hide the panic in her eyes.

"I—" she said, unsure what her next words would be. "I should go to bed. It's late..."

Jackson sat up, lowered his eyes to the roof beneath him, and pulled his hand away, slowly.

"Goodnight, Hannah," he said quietly.

In one fluid motion he leapt from the roof, catching the branch and swinging gently to the ground.

Hannah sat there for a moment, taking deep breaths. When she realized exactly what had just happened, she grimaced and placed her head in her hands.

It didn't matter how great Jackson was.

"*Pretty great...*" she thought.

She was in love with someone else—she was sure of it. Pretty sure, at least. Okay, she was reasonably sure she was in love with someone else. She just couldn't remember whom.

Hannah scooted gingerly off the roof, barely catching the branch below. Then she half swung, half fell to the ground, landing awkwardly on her feet. Tiptoeing into the house, she slipped into her bedroom. Without bothering to wash or change, Hannah climbed into her bed, telling herself over and over again,

"*Remember. You must remember...*"

"You must remember!" came another voice.

Hannah kept her eyes tightly shut.

"Please be the door," she whispered. "Please be the door."

She opened her eyes and breathed a sigh of relief. There she stood in the marble room with the silver door in front of her. She was tired of being afraid. Tired of being uncertain. She wanted answers. And she was going to get them.

She marched straight up to the door and tried to look brave while her shaking hand pulled the key from beneath her shirt. Managing to steady her arm, she bent down and unlocked the door. It made an awful creaking noise as she slowly turned the key—like it was caked in invisible rust and didn't want to open. Then she stepped back, took a deep breath, and asked,

"What must I remember? I need answers."

She turned the handle and pushed the door open, which took all her strength. Then she saw it: her own face staring back at her from the other side of the door. At first, she thought it must be some sort of mirror, so she stretched out her hand. What she felt was not glass, but flesh—warm and very much alive.

Hannah let out the loudest scream her tiny frame could muster and slammed the door as quickly as she could. She crumpled to the ground, pulling her knees to her chest and breathing heavily. She was unsure how long she lay there but the light in the marble room slowly faded, and the next thing she knew she was opening her eyes in her own bed.

"*What...?*"

She pulled herself out of bed, changed her clothes, and managed to stop shaking before she walked into the kitchen and joined the others at the table.

"Good morning!" she called, cheerfully.

She tried to smile at Jackson, but he wouldn't make eye contact with her.

In the end she stared into her teacup for the entirety of breakfast, freaking out internally about Jackson and about the face on the other side of the door—her face.

⌒

Hannah sat at the foot of her bed flipping through the book she had bought Cavan for his birthday.

"Bla bla bla, support beams, bla bla bla, structure joints, bla bla bla...I don't care. Apparently, architecture is not my thing," she said to herself, stashing the book in the drawer of her bedside table.

June had arrived and Cavan's birthday was that evening, so Hannah headed off to Charlotte's shop to get some fabric to wrap his gift. When she got there, she found Kinleigh and Charlotte hard at work.

"I thought we were taking the day off?" she asked curiously, as she selected a small bit of silver cloth from the scrap pile. "Mrs. Ediff collected her dress yesterday. Wasn't that the last order we had for the ball?"

"Last order? Yes," replied Kinleigh.

"Last dress? No," Charlotte added.

Hannah gave them a puzzled look as she stuffed the bit of fabric into her pocket.

"Arms up!" said Kinleigh, marching over to her with a roll of fabric.

"What? No."

"Oh come on, Hannah. Don't be a spoiled sport!"

"I couldn't possibly allow you to make me a dress."

"The thought never crossed my mind. You're making this one yourself."

"What? I couldn't—I mean—I don't even know how—"

"You've been working with us for almost three months now," Charlotte interjected. "You've picked up more than you think."

"Besides," continued Kinleigh, "You won't be completely on your own. I still have my dress to make. We'll go through all the steps together—just do what I do. And we have a whole week to work on it."

"Oh goodness. Well I'm not quite sure I'll be...that is...well I wasn't really planning on attending the ball..." Hannah blurted out.

"Nonsense, dear!" Charlotte replied. "You've been working so hard, you deserve a bit of fun."

Hannah searched her mind for the proper response, but the truth was she couldn't go to the ball. It was being thrown in her cousin's honor at her uncle's palace. And she was, after all, on the run. What if they saw her? Her face turned pale as she thought about all the ramifications of this possibility.

"I—" she started.

"Oh save it, Hannah!" laughed Kinleigh. "Do you really think I'm going to let you miss this? Arms up!"

Hannah obeyed. They draped fabrics around her of various colors and patterns, searching for something extra special for the occasion.

"Oooh! What about this one?!" Kinleigh called, holding up a roll of bright blue silk. "Can you imagine how great this would look with your blonde hair?"

She cringed. "*That's exactly the problem with this whole plan,*" she thought. But then an idea struck her.

"About that..." she said, a grin suddenly taking over her face. "I'm going to need your help with something. And I was thinking..."

She dug through the fabric pile and pulled out a roll that had been tucked away on the very bottom.

"...something more like...this."

CHAPTER 14

MASQUERADE

Prince Damian's birthday had arrived and the whole kingdom of Lemeth had shut down for the occasion. After all, everyone was traveling to Gillodel for the ball. Everyone except for Cavan and Charlotte, that is. Hannah had tried to convince them that if she had to go, so did they, but no amount of begging or coercion made any difference.

"We don't have the best history with dances," they said. And that was that.

The other two, along with Hannah, had set off the morning before the ball and stayed overnight at a small inn just outside the capital city. The girls rose with the sun and began getting ready. Jackson, however, decided it was the perfect morning for a lie in. When he finally got up, he heard the girls giggling in the next room. He knocked on the door and Kinleigh opened it a crack.

"Morning, sleepyhead!" she said, poking fun at her big brother.

He rolled his eyes but smiled.

"Hey, sis. What's with all the noise?"

"Hannah and I are working some magic in here."

Jackson's eyes widened with panic. "Kinleigh! We're not supposed to be—"

"Shh! Calm down," she whispered, stepping quickly into his adjoining room and closing the door behind her.

"That's not what I meant. We're just getting ready for the ball."

He breathed a sigh of relief.

"Oh. You know you really should be more careful with your choice of words."

"And you really shouldn't be so quick to jump to conclusions. I'm not a child anymore. You need to trust me."

Jackson gave her a playful punch in the arm.

"Whatever you say, kid."

"I should get back in there. We're in the middle of a...delicate procedure."

"Are you sure I shouldn't be worried?"

"Promise," she said, laughing. "You'll understand when you see it."

With this, Kinleigh returned to the other room.

"What was that about?" asked Hannah

"Just my brother being my brother," Kinleigh replied, rolling her eyes. "And speaking of my brother... what's the deal with you two?"

"What do you mean?"

"Well you've both been acting really strange lately. Is there something going on that I should know about?"

Ever since that night on the roof, Jackson had been avoiding Hannah. He hadn't meant to, but he didn't know how to act around her, nor she around him. All she really wanted was for things to go back to the way they were before; they had grown quite close and she missed talking to him. It felt like she had known him forever, and that made being away from home a lot easier. But over the past few weeks she'd started feeling rather lonely. And the nightmare had returned.

"No. I mean, not really. Though I think I may have hurt his feelings."

"Is that it? Don't worry, then. Jackson's always been sensitive. He's been through a lot. And ever since..." she trailed off. "Well, anyway. He'll come around. Now, explain to me again how this is supposed to work?"

Hannah's hair was wrapped in an old cloth and caked with a sticky brown mud-like substance. She was sitting on a bench next to an open window.

"Well apparently if you mix the right clays and spices together, and then put them on your hair for long enough, it will act as a sort of mask. It changes the color for a few days and then washes out.

"And why is your head practically out the window?"

"I think the sunlight is supposed to help it take better."

"You think? Haven't you ever done this before?"

"Of course! Well, sort of. Not exactly. I know someone else who did it one time. Does that count?"

"Well, it definitely counts as insanity, if that's what you mean," Kinleigh said, laughing.

The pair spent the next few hours finishing Hannah's hair, applying the makeup they'd purchased in town the day before, and getting into their gowns.

"Hannah, you look stunning," Kinleigh said, as she helped her lace up the back of her gown. "You did such an amazing job. No one would ever guess this was your first dress."

"Thanks. You look great, too."

Kinleigh grinned.

"And now for the finishing touch..." she added, digging through her bag.

"Finishing touch?"

Just then there was a knock at the door.

"Can I come in?" came Jackson's voice from the other room.

"Yeah!" Kinleigh called back, still rummaging in the bag.

Jackson walked in and started to say something, but when he looked up and saw Hannah, he stopped short of the first word. Her hair, which was now a rich shade of deep brown, was pinned atop her head in ringlets, with a few curls falling just past her ears. The fabric she had chosen for her dress was vibrant crimson. It was cinched at the waist and cascaded from her hips into layers and layers of fabric, which parted at the front. Underneath the layers of gathered red peeked a shimmering golden fabric, similar to tulle, which caused the skirt of the dress to poof out like a rose in full bloom. On her lips was a golden cream that matched the bottom layer of her dress.

He stared at her breathlessly for what seemed like an eternity. Then he noticed Kinleigh, who was standing behind her, pull something out of her bag.

"Aha! There you are!"

"Where's your mask?" Jackson asked, turning back to Hannah.

"...my mask?" questioned the princess.

"You do know this is a masquerade, right?"

Hannah's eyes widened.

"Apparently she didn't," Kinleigh replied.

Hannah turned around to look at Kinleigh. She stopped for a second to admire how lovely her friend looked; she was naturally beautiful but Hannah had never seen her in a dress, let alone in any makeup. Her hair was braided like a crown atop her head and adorned with tiny white flowers. The bright green color of her dress made her eyes sparkle, and her lips were blood red. Now that she was all done up, she reminded the princess of someone. But she couldn't put her finger on it.

Then she noticed the white mask Kinleigh was wearing that covered the top half of her face. Her eyes widened in panic.

"I guess I missed that bit of information," she said, sheepishly. She felt foolish. How could she not have known it was a masquerade? It was her own cousin's birthday celebration, and she didn't know anything about it.

"Where's your mask, then?" she asked Jackson?

He pulled a red mask out from his back pocket and grinned at her.

She smiled back, sighing.

"Don't worry about it, Hannah," said Kinleigh, cheerfully. We'll figure something out. Now if only we had a solution for this train wreck over here," she added, pointing to her brother.

"Hey, what's wrong with the way I look?"

"Nothing...if you're going out to work the farm with Father."

"Be nice!" he replied, laughing. "Besides, Mom made me these clothes special for the ball."

"Your clothes are fine," said his sister. "It's your hair I'm worried about. It's just sort of sticking up on top of your head."

"This is what my hair looks like!"

"Okay, hold on," Hannah interrupted. "I think I can help."

She went to the water basin and wet her hands. Then she scooped a tiny bit of the darkest clay she had used to stain her hair. She rubbed her hands together and ran them through Jackson's hair.

"There you go, that's better," Hannah said, drying her hands on a cloth from the table.

His hair was now slicked back and had the slightest wave running through it toward his left ear.

"Now you're ready for a ball!" Kinleigh responded, with a nod of approval. "Well then, we should be going. We don't want to be late."

Kinleigh led the way out of the room. Hannah started to follow her but Jackson put his hand on her shoulder, squeezing it softly to let her know things were okay between them. That was something she loved about their friendship—it didn't always require words. She crinkled her nose at him and took the mask from him, placing it on his face. It ran vertically, covering the left half of his face from his ear to the middle of his nose. His perfect little button nose.

"Right..." Jackson said after a minute, clearing his throat. " Shall we?"

He offered her his arm. She took it, and they followed Kinleigh outside.

CHAPTER 15

UNDER THE FIRE SKY

It was a mile walk from the inn to the heart of Gillodel, and the ball began at sundown. The plan was to arrive in town a bit early and spend an hour or so exploring before the ball itself. While everywhere else in Lemeth had shut down, the streets of Gillodel were never more alive than the days of great celebrations at the palace. The whole village was abuzz with lavishly dressed people and merchants trying to sell them things. They passed a cart full of exotic foods that even Hannah had never seen before.

"All the way from the shores of Tardyn!" yelled the merchant.

Hannah had always dreamed about one day seeing the kingdom of Tardyn, and its dark castle overlooking the tempestuous Denberlaé Sea. It was said there were mermaids living there, a long time ago, but no one had seen them for ages. Perhaps they were there still, hiding somewhere in the depths of the sea. But she guessed that they had disappeared when the magic did, many years ago.

"Would you like to buy some, miss?" the merchant asked, pulling her back out of her daze.

"Oh. No. No, thank you," she said and pushed her way through the crowd, catching up to her friends who had stopped a few carts ahead of her.

"I have a present for you," Jackson said when she reached them. "Close your eyes."

She looked at him questioningly but did as he said.

"Okay, open!"

When she opened her eyes Jackson was holding the most beautiful mask the princess had ever seen. It was painted gold with a cluster of red gems on one side.

"Oh my!" she gasped. "Oh, it's beautiful!"

"It's yours."

She smiled up at him, a sparkle in her blue eyes.

"After all, we couldn't be seen in public with the fool who didn't bring a mask to a masquerade."

He winked as he said this and placed the mask gently on her face.

Then he grabbed Hannah with one hand and Kinleigh with the other, and they made their way through the throngs of people toward the palace.

❧

Hannah stared at the castle intently as they approached. It had been years since she had last seen this sight, and she'd forgotten just how beautiful it was. The light grey stone stood out in stark contrast to the palate of colors in the sky behind it; the sunset had painted it a hundred shades of red, pink, and gold. The stars were just beginning to peek through and they looked like thousands of tiny embers setting the sky on fire.

Her parents were visiting Lemeth when Queen Gwyneria discovered she was pregnant. She used to tell her daughter,

"You were made under the fire sky of Gillodel and born of the embers that sparked it. That is why we named you Emberlynn."

You see, Gillodel was the only place in the world with a view like that. The stars that shone above the palace never moved. Other stars moved around them as the seasons changed, but the stars of Gillodel were always constant. This was another of Hannah's favorite stories from her childhood. Snow White had sat on the throne of Lemeth hundreds of years before. It was said that when her prince kissed her to wake her from the witch's curse, that kiss sent an explosion of sparks into the sky, burning white with the flame of true love, which can never be extinguished. Those sparks sat forever above the palace where Snow White ruled, watching over them and protecting her kingdom and her people.

Hannah had always felt a longing for ages past, where love was true and magic was alive. It had faded over long centuries until almost nothing remained. She almost wondered if it hadn't disappeared entirely. Some said the fairies still lived in the Forest of Ćerianell, south of Gillodel just beyond the shore of the Tavys River. Her grandfather had had dealings with the fairies (she knew the story of the necklace they made for her grandmother) but no one she knew had seen them since.

"Are you coming, Hannah?" Kinleigh called to her.

Hannah came back to her senses and found herself standing at the base of the palace steps. She took in a deep breath.

"Even if the magic is gone, I have a feeling tonight is still going to be magical," she thought.

She expelled the breath from her lungs, and all of her fears with it. Then she picked up the bottom of her dress and followed Jackson and Kinleigh, who were halfway up the steps by this point.

They followed the crowd into the palace, marveling at its beauty. Hannah ran her hands over the cool stone column by the door, brushed the great tapestry as she passed it, and as she rounded the corner into the great hall a flood of memories came rushing back.

The main banquet table had been cleared out of the hall to accommodate the guests, but when she closed her eyes, she saw it clearly in the center of the room. She sat beside her mother in a blue dress, fidgeting with the bow around her waist. Gwyneria leaned in and whispered for her to sit still at the table. Then she stroked her daughter's hair and kissed the top of her head.

Hannah smiled and opened her eyes. That night the hall was filled with people, with more spread throughout the whole western wing of the palace. Everyone was dressed in their finest apparel—most of the women wearing new dresses they'd purchased for the occasion. Seeing the size of the crowd made her more relieved than ever to be wearing a mask. Between that and her dark hair she knew even her relatives wouldn't recognize her unless they were standing right in front of her.

Upon further examination she noticed the two smaller tables had been left in the hall but had been pushed to the sides against opposite walls. They were topped with breads, pastries, aged cheese, fine wine, and an array of other appetizing things.

"Let's have a look at that table, shall we?" she said to her friends.

"I had the very same idea," Jackson replied.

They weaved their way through the crowd to the other side of the room and were just about to sample a bit of asiago when there was a loud knocking sound, and a sudden hush fell over the crowd. Hannah recognized it as the sound of the herald banging his staff upon the ground to quiet the crowd. She turned around and saw her uncle and his wife, Queen Alette, standing atop a raised dais that had been constructed for the occasion. Most balls were held in the throne room, but since the whole kingdom had been invited to this one, they had to use the banquet hall, which was much larger.

"*Now that I think of it,*" she thought, "*it is a bit odd that they invited the entire kingdom to celebrate Damian's birthday. They usually only do that when...oh my,*" she trailed off, coming to a sudden realization. "*How could I have been so stupid? Why didn't I realize that before? Well this is an occasion!*"

"Thank you all for coming tonight!" King Thomas began. "It touches my heart to see how fond you all are of my only son, Damian."

Loud cheers.

"And, of course, of a nice ball," he joked.

Laughter.

"Hannah, why are you smiling?" asked Jackson, noticing the look on his friend's face.

She put her finger to her lips, grinning.

"As you all know, today is his twenty-first birthday."

More cheers.

"Yes, yes. I am quite proud of the man he's become, and proud to have him as my son. And tonight I have an announcement which also makes a father's heart proud."

Silence.

Hannah caught Jackson's eye and nodded. He gave her a questioning look then turned back to the dais.

"It gives us great pleasure to announce," he said, taking his wife by the hand, "the engagement of our son Damian to Princess Sierra of Tardyn!"

The crowd continued in stunned silence for a moment then burst forth in cheers of "Huzzah!" and "Many happy returns!"

If there was one thing the people of Lemeth liked more than a good ball, it was a royal wedding.

Then came the loud knock again.

"We're so glad you share in our excitement for this wonderful news. Unfortunately the princess was unable to be here tonight as we had hoped. She was called away unexpectedly a few days ago, due to the sudden illness of her father. She returned to Tardyn to help care for him, but we expect her back in Gillodel as soon as he has recovered. Now, please," he said, motioning to the musicians, "that's enough talking and more than enough to celebrate. Let the dancing begin!"

With that the music started. Many people found a partner and took their place on the floor. Others withdrew to the side of the room to continue conversations or to indulge themselves at the tables. Hannah picked up the piece of asiago she had been eyeing and popped the whole thing into her mouth.

"You knew what King Thomas was going to say, didn't you?" asked Jackson.

Hannah stared at him and continued to chew the large chunk of cheese in her mouth.

"How did you know Damian was engaged? It doesn't seem like anyone in all of Lemeth knew that."

When she finally swallowed, she looked him in the eye and said, "We all have our secrets."

They both smiled.

"Isn't that right, Kinleigh? Kin...Kinleigh?"

They looked around but saw no sign of her. Jackson was beginning to panic when he finally caught sight of her dancing with a stranger in a blue mask. Kinleigh saw them and waved timidly with one hand. Jackson laughed with relief. His sister rolled her eyes and turned back to her partner.

"Well now that I know my sister hasn't been hurt, poisoned, or...taken by wolves," said Jackson, dramatically, with a sweep of his hand, "I can enjoy this fine feast."

He picked up a pastry that looked like it was filled with bit of apple. After eying it hungrily he moved it toward his mouth.

At that moment Hannah felt a chill run down her spine. She froze, and from the corner of her eye she saw a man approaching the table. He was dressed in all black, including the mask that covered most of his face. But his blue eyes pierced through in sharp contrast to the black surrounding them. The princess would know those eyes anywhere.

Banning.

"*What is he doing here?*" she thought, completely taken by surprise.

Her heart was stuck in her throat, and she knew she had only seconds to act. In one awkward but effective move she grabbed Jackson's hand, knocking the pastry from it, and pulled him toward the dance floor.

"Hey!" he objected. "I was going to eat that! Did you see how delicious that looked? What—"

He stopped short when he noticed the look of panic on Hannah's face.

"Hannah, what's wrong?"

She was as pale as the grave and gripped his hand like it was the only thing tying her to life. Jackson pulled her close as they reached the corner of the dance floor and began swaying slowly to the music.

"What's wrong?" he asked again, quietly. "Your hands are shaking."

"I..." she managed, as she slowly recovered her breath. "I...I'm fine. I just. I'm sorry, I really can't tell you."

She pulled away from him slowly.

"It's okay, you don't have to. But whatever it is, it's okay now. I won't let anything happen to you. You know that, right?"

He pulled her back to him and they resumed dancing.

"I know," she whispered, pressing her head into his chest. "I know."

The song ended and was followed by an up-tempo number. Jackson spun Hannah and turned around quickly himself, grabbing her hand as it came back around and leading her to the center of the dance floor.

"I didn't know you could dance," Hannah said.

"There's a lot you don't know about me."

"Such as…?"

"We all have our—"

"Secrets?" she asked, cutting him off.

Jackson laughed merrily. He spun her again, and as she turned she collided with the person behind her, knocking her mask to the ground.

"I'm so sorry," said a familiar voice.

She looked up and found herself face to face with Damian. His face was covered by a bright blue mask but she knew her cousin well enough to pick him out of a crowd, even at a masquerade. He bent down to pick her mask up off the floor and held it out to her.

"Thank you," she said, quietly, trying to disguise her voice.

The prince stared at her intently and, as he did so, a light began to grow in his eyes. This was it—a few more seconds and her secret would be out. She grabbed the mask from him, curtseyed, and ran as fast as she could to the exit. She had just enough time to notice the girl standing beside him—the one he had been dancing with when they collided.

It was Kinleigh.

CHAPTER 16

AT FIRST SIGHT

Jackson followed Hannah out of the great hall, grabbing an apple pastry from the table as he passed it.

"You really are on edge tonight, Hannah," he said, when he caught up to her. "I've never seen you like this."

"Tonight is turning out to be everything I hoped it wouldn't."

She knew it wasn't a good answer but it was the only one she had to give. He looked at her with a light of understanding in his eyes, and that scared her.

"Come with me," he said, with the strangest look on his face.

"Where are we going?"

"It seems to me that you could use some fresh air."

He took her by the hand and led her outside. They walked a little way from the door, then turned a corner. Standing before them were the royal gardens. The smell of roses greeted them, beckoning them inward with thousands of tiny lights.

"Snowberries," she whispered, not sure where the word came from.

"What?"

"Those lights. They're Snowberries, aren't they? At least I think that's what they're called."

"Yes. They are. Do you know why?"

Hannah's head felt fuzzy, like a fog was forming inside her mind.

"I think maybe I do, but I can't remember."

"Well, then. Let me tell you."

He sat down on a bench on the edge of the garden and motioned for her to join him. She did, and he continued.

"Once upon a time Snow White and her prince sat upon the throne of Lemeth. And everyone knows, they lived happily ever after. But that wasn't always the case. Long before she took the throne, Snow White fled from the palace in fear for her life..."

He paused and looked her in the eye when he said this; a knot formed in the pit of her stomach. After a moment he continued.

"You see, people sometimes think that just because a person joins the court of the king they are good; that they can be trusted. But that's not always true."

He paused again. Hannah's heart began racing and the fog started forming in her head again. Jackson seemed to sense her discomfort and confusion. He furrowed his brow and sighed. Then he smiled at her and said, "But you already know that part of the story, I'm sure."

She stared at him.

"With the wicked stepmother?" he added.

"Oh, yeah. And the apple..." she said, nodding toward his pastry.

"Oh, I'm definitely going to eat this. I didn't get my other one!" He nudged her playfully. "Besides, I highly doubt King Thomas plans to poison the guests at his son's engagement ball."

Hannah laughed.

"So I know about the curse, and the kiss and the stars. But what does that have to do with the Snowberries?"

"Well, on the day of Snow White's wedding the stars rained down a silver-golden light upon the palace. It soaked into the ground of the garden and from that light grew the Snowberries. They were named for—"

"Snow White," Hannah finished.

"Exactly."

Jackson bent down and picked one from a small cluster near the bench and handed it to Hannah. It was cold to the touch, despite the warm summer evening. She put it in her mouth and found herself standing in the same garden, many years before, in a pale pink dress. The garden was shrouded in a dense fog. She had a fistful of Snowberries and could taste them on her tongue.

"These are delicious!" came a voice from behind her. It belonged to a young boy about her age; she could just make him out through the fog.

"I can't believe you've never tasted Snowberries before!" she found herself saying.

"Well, your uncle's palace is the only place you can find them. And it isn't exactly open to the public," he laughed.

"Well I'm not the public," she replied, laughing as well. "Nor are you," she added. And she meant it.

Then she saw it, a shadow coming up behind the boy through the fog. She put her fingers to her lips, dropping the handful of Snowberries as she did so. Then she motioned quickly for him to follow her as she hid behind a large rosebush. The pair had just crouched down out of view when the figure passed by. Another followed closely behind.

"Well? Hannah? Hannah?!"

She opened her eyes and found herself once again sitting beside Jackson.

"Well? How was it?"

"Delicious," she replied. "Uh, Jackson?"

"Yeah?"

"Do you think we could maybe have a look round the rest of the garden?"

He stood, smiling, and helped her to her feet. Then the pair set off to explore the garden. They passed through a large grove of trees and when they reached the other side Hannah gasped. In the very center of the garden stood a giant fountain bubbling over with the clearest water she had ever seen. It was made of pure silver and both the fountain and the water reflected the starlight, making it shine like it was a star itself.

The princes walked over to the fountain and dipped her hand in the water. It was ice cold and sent a shiver through her whole body. She sneezed twice, from the cold, then bent down to wipe her hand on the grass.

"That's freezing!"

"Then you better come away from there before you fall in."

She nodded and backed away. They continued walking and had almost reached the western edge of the garden when they heard footsteps. Someone was coming. Hannah didn't know if they were allowed to be in the garden, and she certainly wasn't looking to have a heart-to-heart chat with members of the Lemethian guard. Apparently, Jackson was thinking the same thing because he quickly moved behind another dense cluster of trees, pulling Hannah along with him. But when the owner of the footsteps came into view it wasn't a guard. It was Damian—and Kinleigh was with him.

"You have got to be kidding me!" they whispered in unison.

This made them giggle, but they quickly quieted down again and listened as the pair began to talk.

"Are we supposed to be out here?" questioned Kinleigh.

"I don't think it will be a problem," was the response.

"Oh, she doesn't know," Hannah whispered.

"Doesn't know what?" asked Jackson.

"Who that is," answered Emberlynn, pointing to the man in the blue mask.

"Well it is a masquerade. That's kind of the point."

"Oh. Oh, you don't know either. Oh my."

"'Oh my,' what?"

Hannah grinned sheepishly.

"So far you're two for two on knowing things that nobody else here knows," he continued. "Well, are you going to tell me who's cavorting with my little sister or aren't you?"

"I don't think I'm going to have to," she said, nodding toward the cavorters.

Jackson looked and saw the man slowly removing his mask. He turned to Hannah in wide-eyed disbelief.

On the other side of the trees, Kinleigh was having the same reaction.

"You...You're..." she stammered.

"I know."

"No, but you're really—"

"I know."

"But they just announced your..." Kinleigh trailed off.

"Yes, right. I actually sort of forgot about that."

"Forgot? About your own fiancé?"

"At least I was trying to."

She gave him a look of disgusted disbelief and backed away slowly.

"No, I'm sorry! Wait! I'm sorry, that came out wrong."

She sat down on a nearby bench and put her hands in her head.

"We've been dancing all night. And talking. And...I thought..."

He sat down next to her, placing a hand on her shoulder. She looked up and said,

"I told my brother this morning that I'm not a child anymore, but maybe I was wrong. Maybe I am—a silly, childish girl who gave her heart to a man in a mask, without even knowing his name."

"You weren't wrong. About your brother or about...what you thought."

"But how can that be? You're a prince. And you're engaged. How could you possibly—"

"I don't love her!" he blurted out. "I never have."

"Then why...?"

"It's my father. And her father as well. They believe 'an alliance of the highest sort will benefit and strengthen both kingdoms,'" he said, in a mocking tone. "Or at least that's what my father keeps saying."

"Don't you have a say in the matter?"

"No. Nor does she."

"You mean she doesn't love you either?"

"We barely know each other. I tried to change my father's mind, but he said I couldn't form a strong enough argument against it and the good it would bring to our kingdom would be worth the sacrifice."

"But he's not the one making the sacrifice."

"Well other people's sacrifices are always the easiest ones to make. But the truth is this is how things have always been done, at least for the past age. The stories of true love overcoming all obstacles... those are all in history books. And have you ever noticed how many of them involved royalty falling in love with royalty? If I'd fallen in love with another royal my father would have let me marry for love. Maybe if I'd fallen in love at all; at least I like to think that would have been a good enough reason for him. But now it's too late to find out."

"Then it's a good thing there's no such thing as love at first sight," Kinleigh said, with a small laugh.

"There might be. Should we find out...?"

With this he reached up to remove her mask.

"This has gone far enough!" Jackson whispered. He was about to step out from behind the trees when Hannah grabbed him by the shoulders and pulled him back.

"That's my sister out there!"

"Yes, and that's my....prince," she said awkwardly, stopping herself just as the word "cousin" was forming on her tongue.

"I thought you were from Ardia?" he said.

"I...Oh, shut up. You can't just barge out there."

"Why not?"

"*Well, for starters he can't see me because I'm his cousin and he can't know I'm here!*" she thought.

"Well for starters, if you go out there now, they'll know we've been listening the entire time."

"Oh."

"And as a follow up reason, he's the prince and he could call the royal guard on us, sister or no sister."

"Oh, fine!" he said, finally. "But it's really important that he doesn't take her mask off."

"Why?"

"Just... just trust me. This is one of those 'I can't tell you' things."

"Ok well we've got about ten seconds so...."

Jackson bent down, picked up a rock, and threw it toward Damian and Kinleigh.

"Ouch! What was—?" asked Damian.

The rock had hit him in the back of the head.

"I thought you wanted to stop the prince, not injure him," laughed Hannah.

"I wasn't aiming for him, okay? I just—oh shut up and run!"

While Jackson hadn't meant to hit Damian, he had at least achieved the desired result. Damian stopped before he'd taken off Kinleigh's mask. Unfortunately they were now heading right toward Hannah and Jackson.

"Where exactly are we running to?" she asked.

"I don't know. We're just running."

After a minute they could see the very edge of the garden. There were guards at the gate, the wall of the palace in front of them, and a very startled prince behind them.

"What now?" asked Jackson.

"Why are you asking me?"

"Hey I came up with that rock idea. It's your turn."

Hannah was about to tell him she didn't have any ideas when something caught her eye. There was a large ivy vine growing up the side of the castle. Behind it she saw the faintest glow, like something reflecting the starlight.

"Follow me!" she whispered.

They could hear the footsteps closing in behind them. Hannah took a deep breath and crawled behind the ivy. She ran her hand along the stone until she found what she was looking for. Then she pushed as hard as she could. Suddenly the wall opened up, revealing a small stone door in the side of the castle.

"What in the world?"

"Just come on!"

They squeezed through the door and shut it most of the way, leaving a crack just big enough to peek through.

"Well, whoever it was they're gone now," came Damian's voice.

"I guess it's just as well," said Kinleigh. "We should probably be getting back to the ball. It is your ball, after all."

"You're probably right," Damian sighed. "Will you at least tell me your name?"

"Kinleigh."

"Hello, Kinleigh," he said, taking her hand and kissing it.

With that, they left the garden and went back inside.

"Good girl," breathed Jackson, with a sigh of relief. "Now, explain to me how you were able to open a door in the side of the castle."

"Structure joints," she said, matter-of-factly.

"Structure what?"

"It's something I read in the architecture book I got for your father. You can sometimes locate a hidden door by looking for signs of the joint."

"Seriously, what?"

"They have to use some sort of mechanism to attach and move the entrance. One side typically has a near-invisible metal joint. I saw the light reflecting off of it behind the ivy."

"Okay, I am really impressed."

"Don't be," she laughed. "That's the only thing I remember from that book, and I barely understand it."

"Well they're gone now. Should we get out of here?"

Hannah wanted to say yes. She wanted to go back inside, grab Kinleigh, and drag her back to the inn. She wanted to go back to Cavan and Charlotte's where she knew she would be safe, to hide away and escape the suffocating fog that was taking over her mind. She wanted to, but she couldn't.

"I think we should see where this passage leads," she said instead, motioning to the tunnel leading beyond them into the castle.

"I was hoping you'd say that," Jackson grinned. "Come on."

He pulled the garden door shut behind them then headed down the tunnel, Hannah at his heels.

CHAPTER 17

CHRONICLES OF THE KINGDOM

"Do you see anything?" Hannah whispered.

"I'm not sure. It's really dark in here."

"Well, yes, I noticed."

"Wait, I think I see a light up ahead."

They followed the passage around a small bend in the tunnel and found themselves standing in front of a great wooden wall. There was a faint line of light coming from the other side which allowed them to see the outline of the door. Seeing a small lever, Jackson reached up to pull it.

"This wasn't part of the plan," came a voice from the other side of the wall.

Jackson stopped and pulled his hand away quickly.

"Plans change. The important thing is not that things always go according to plan, rather that you know how take advantage of those changes to make things turn out your way in the end," came a second voice.

"And how do you propose we take advantage of this particular change? Emberlynn is gone and now a Tardynian princess is to have the throne of Gillodel."

Hannah's eyes widened and she pressed her ear to the door. Jackson did the same.

"That's how the game is played, my boy. Sometimes you have to sacrifice your queen in order to check the king."

"And when your queen is gone, what do you use to check the king?"

"That's what pawns are for."

There was a pause in the conversation, and they heard the sound of rustling paper.

"You can't be serious."

"You know what they say about desperate times."

"Are we really that desperate?"

"No. No, I supposed not. Not yet anyway. But one more surprise and we may be out of options."

The first man had no reply.

"It's getting late. We should return downstairs and catch the end of the festivities. You know how I love a good ball."

When the sound of their footsteps had disappeared Hannah reached up and pulled the lever. The door creaked open and she walked through it.

"Hannah, be careful!" whispered Jackson.

"It's fine. They're gone."

He followed her through the door and found himself standing in the middle of a giant room. Shelves upon shelves of books, reaching to the ceiling, covered the walls.

"This must be the library," he said.

Hannah nodded. Then something caught her eye. In the middle of the room was a large table. On top of it she saw a large book. She recognized that book. It was the same one she'd been flipping through at the bookshop in Faryn—the one with the missing page. *Chronicles of the Kingdoms.*

She walked over to it and found it lying open to the last page.

Prince Aedyn *of Ardia.*

When she saw the picture she gasped audibly and stepped back, placing her hand over her mouth. Staring back at her was the face she had seen in her dream on the other side of the strange silver door. Her face—only it wasn't.

Prince Aedyn is the first son of King Edric and Queen Gwyneria of Ardia. He is first in line for the throne of Ardia, followed by his twin sister, Emberlynn.

"What?! No! No."

"What's wrong, Hannah?" asked Jackson, walking toward her.

She quickly closed the book, hoping he wouldn't notice.

"If I ask you a question will you promise not to ask me a bunch in return about why I don't know the answer?"

He gave her a questioning look but said, "Yes. Of course."

"Jackson..." she said. "What happened to Prince Aedyn of Ardia?"

His eyes widened and he looked as if he'd just been punched. He opened his mouth to answer but stopped himself. Instead he looked intently into her eyes for a moment and she was unable to guess what he might be thinking.

"I wish I could tell you," he said finally.

"You mean no one knows?"

"Well, no, not really."

"How is it possible that a person can disappear and people not remember—I mean know...people not know what happened to him?"

"That's the big question. He just went missing one day, right from under the noses of his family, the royal guard...everyone."

"And they have no idea what happened?"

He paused again, mulling something over in his mind.

"A young nobleman was accused of kidnapping him. There was no real proof, of course. But they found someone to blame it on and they weren't going to let that go."

"What happened to him?"

"He was exiled. Since they couldn't prove it, they couldn't execute him. Or maybe the king just wouldn't. He had been a close friend of King Thomas before it all happened."

"Wait, King Thomas? I thought Aedyn was prince of Ardia?"

"He was. But the royal family of Ardia was visiting Gillodel when he disappeared."

Hannah's head was reeling. She was standing in the palace where her brother disappeared—a brother she couldn't even remember having. It was too much for her to handle so she did the only natural thing for a person to do at a time like this: she fainted.

When Hannah opened her eyes, she was lying on a hard, wooden floor in a dimly lit room. Jackson was sitting beside her.

"What...?" she said, foggily. "What happened?"

"You fainted," replied Jackson, looking both concerned and amused. "Here..."

He stood up and helped Hannah to her feet.

"Are you alright?"

"Yeah, I think so. Everything just went fuzzy for a moment."

"Well it's been a long night. And if I recall you've only had a small bit of cheese since we got here."

"Yeah, we should probably head downstairs and have a bite to eat before the ball ends. It should be over soon."

"I'm heading straight for the apple tarts."

"You've had two already!" Hannah said, laughing.

"No, I've only had one. You smacked the first one away from me, remember?"

"Fair enough. Let's—"

Hannah stopped suddenly in the middle of her thought.

"What's the matter?" asked Jackson.

She had been so busy looking at the book on the table that she'd failed to notice the object lying beside it.

A large black mask.

Hannah froze.

"Everything."

All of a sudden, they heard footsteps approaching the library.

"Run!" she whispered.

"Haven't we done enough of that tonight?" complained Jackson. But he followed her back through the hidden door, shutting it behind him. They ran back down the tunnel, raced from the garden, and headed into the castle, breathing heavily.

"You know, dresses like this..." panted Hannah, "they were not made for running."

They walked slowly into the great hall, pressing through the crowd of people still merrying the night away. Hannah went straight to the table at the entrance and grabbed a goblet of water, which she drank thirstily. Jackson put his hand on her shoulder and, when she looked at him, gave her a questioning look.

She nodded to let him know she was okay—even though she wasn't.

☙

Back in the library, Banning had returned to get his mask. He grabbed it from the table and placed it back upon his face. He was just turning to leave when he stopped suddenly.

"Father!" he called, panic in his voice.

"What is it?" asked the duke, running into the room.

"I think someone has been here."

"What do you mean?"

"The book on the table—I don't remember closing it."

Theron let out a sigh of relief.

"That's not possible, Banning. We hadn't gone that far down the hall before you turned back to get your mask. And this is the only door. Anyone coming to the library would have had to pass us to get here."

"I suppose you're right. I guess I'm just being paranoid."

The pair was heading back down the hall when Theron stopped and put his hand on Banning's shoulder.

"All the same..." he said, sternly. "In the future, always close the book. And remember the mask. We can't afford to get careless."

With that he resumed walking—down the hallway, back down the stairs, and into the great hall, with Banning at his heels. They both found a pretty partner to share the last few dances with, then said their goodbyes to the king and queen before heading home to Whitehawk Estate.

It had been a long night for everyone.

Chapter 18

THE UNANSWERED QUESTION

That night Hannah didn't sleep; she lay awake in her bed at the inn as Kinleigh slept soundly beside her. She was grateful that neither Kinleigh nor Jackson had been very talkative on the walk back from the palace. They were all still processing the events of the evening and they mostly walked in silence. And now she was alone with her thoughts.

Her mind raced circles around one name: Aedyn. The name she had read in the Chronicles of the Kingdoms. The face she had seen on the other side of the door. Her brother? But how could that be? There were so many pieces to the puzzle in her head and the more pieces she uncovered, the less clearly those pieces seemed to fit together. Or were they chess pieces? Banning and Theron had spoken of a chess game, and all the things and people with which they were playing.

"Emberlynn is gone," she heard Banning's words in her head.

"Sometimes you have to sacrifice your queen..."

She shuddered.

So she was the queen—a piece in a dark game that Theron and Banning were playing. A piece to be sacrificed and discarded when she was no longer of use to them. This didn't surprise her all that much, really. After all, hadn't that been the very reason she left? She didn't trust Banning.

But what of her brother? How was he to be used as a pawn?

"*They know something about his disappearance,*" she thought. "*They must. But how?*"

She knew one thing for certain: Theron and Banning were up to something, and it most likely involved a plot to overthrow her father or uncle...or both.

She needed to find out more—about this plan, about her past, about her brother—but where did she start? She knew the answer to this question even as she asked it. She pulled the key out from under her nightdress and turned it in her hand. Then she took a deep breath and closed her eyes. As the first rays of sunlight fell on her face she began fading into a deep sleep. She was just beginning to feel the cool marble materializing beneath her when she heard a voice.

"Good morning, Hannah," yawned Kinleigh, as she rolled over beside her in the large bed.

Hannah's eyes shot open and she sat up, feeling completely disoriented.

"What? Oh, yeah. Hi—errr—good morning...Kins." She blinked a few times to clear her vision as she found her head again.

"Uh, yeah..." said Kinleigh, giving her a questioning look. "You okay?"

"What? Oh, yeah...yeah, sorry. Sorry, I was just having a very...vivid dream."

"What about?" she asked, sitting up next to Hannah.

"Darkness."

"Vivid darkness?'

Hannah nodded.

"That's a strange thing to be dreaming about."

"Not strange," said Hannah, slowly, "just incomplete."

Kinleigh was about to ask her what she meant when there was a knock at the door.

"Come on, sleepyheads!" came Jackson's voice. "Let's grab breakfast, then head home. We've a long walk ahead of us."

"The sun's only just opened its eyes!" Kinleigh called back. "How can you expect us to have opened ours?"

The girls dressed swiftly, gathered their belongings and met Jackson downstairs for breakfast. They ate quickly then headed back to Faryn.

The journey was mostly a silent one—everyone lost in his own thoughts. Hannah replayed the events of the previous night over and over in her mind. At the center of it was one pressing question.

"Hey Jackson...?" she said quietly, walking a little faster so she was right beside him.

"Yeah?"

"Do you think Prince Aedyn is still alive?"

He was silent for a moment.

"Honestly, I don't know what I think. I certainly hope he is, but it's been five years."

Hannah froze, using all her energy in a simple effort to keep the air moving in and out of her lungs.

"Are you okay, Hannah?"

"Five... five years?" she managed, after a minute.

"Almost to the day. It was the celebration of Prince Damian's sixteenth birthday. This is the first ball that has been held at the palace of Gillodel since that night."

"What are you two on about?" asked Kinleigh, catching up to them.

"Just waiting on you, slowpoke," Jackson laughed, nudging his sister.

She rolled her eyes but smiled.

"Well come on then. I'm here now."

They resumed walking but Hannah's head was still spinning.

"Hannah..." Jackson said softly, seeing the sadness in her eyes. "I think if he were not alive, we surely would have known by now. I have hope. I always have."

He smiled at her then walked on ahead, catching up with his sister.

Hannah followed, a fire growing in her. She knew what was in that marble room behind the silver door. She had no idea why, or how it was even possible, but she knew it all the same. That's where she'd been headed when Kinleigh woke her—to the room in her head, the door in her dreams, and the face behind it.

Before she knew it, they were back home at the cottage. The sun was just beginning to set as they walked through the door.

"How was the ball?" asked Charlotte, who was in the process of setting the table for supper.

There was a brief pause, as none of them wanted to give an honest answer.

"It was really nice," said Kinleigh, finally.

"Good!"

"They announced the prince's engagement," she added, quietly.

"Engagement?" questioned Cavan, coming in from the other room. "To whom?"

"The princess of Tardyn," answered Jackson.

The two exchanged a worried look which Hannah, who was deep in thought, did not notice.

"How nice for Prince Damian," said Charlotte, after a moment. "Well, you're just in time for dinner. Wash up and we can eat."

After dinner Cavan helped Charlotte with the dishes and sent the others to bed.

"You've had a long day and it's back to work tomorrow. Get some rest."

If Hannah had been paying attention as she headed to her room, she would have heard Charlotte whisper, "Should we be worried?"

"I don't know if we should be, but I admit that I am," was Cavan's reply.

"What do we do?"

"We keep our distance. There's nothing else we can do."

But Hannah was not paying attention and heard none of this.

She did, however, hear a soft thump above her head just as she was climbing into bed. She smiled and put her feet back on the floor. Very carefully she tiptoed her way through the dark kitchen and slipped outside. It was a warm summer night and the sky was full of stars. She walked around the side of the house and climbed up the tree onto the roof. This was a difficult task since she was wearing her nightgown, but she managed it.

Jackson smiled at her as she sat down beside him.

"I think this might be my favorite spot in the whole kingdom," he said. "I feel like nothing can touch me up here. And it's so beautiful."

He lay down on his back and Hannah did the same.

"I wish I felt that way," sighed Hannah. "Wherever I am I feel...exposed. Like someone's watching me. Like nowhere is ever really safe."

Jackson pulled Hannah close to him and wrapped his arms around her.

"Hannah, you are my friend and I will always keep you safe."

She lay her head down on his chest and remembered, for the first time in months, what safe felt like.

"Jackson?"

"Hmmm?"

"Can I ask you something?"

"Of course."

"If there was something, some answer to a question or piece of a puzzle, and you knew once you had that answer it would change your life forever...would you still want to know?"

Jackson thought about this for a minute.

"I guess it would depend on the question."

"What if it was something big; something important? And you might be the only one who could unlock that answer."

"Then I would ask myself what I was more afraid of: facing that change, or living the rest of my life under the weight of a big, important, infinite question."

"And what would you tell yourself?"

"Not to let anything stand between me and that answer. If you alone hold the key to unlocking some great mystery, then maybe that's what you were born to do. And if that's the case, then whatever lies on the other side of that change is your destiny. And that is an intimidating thought, I know. But I don't think there's anything quite as frightening as the unanswered question."

Hannah pondered this in the silence that followed and fell asleep to the sound of Jackson's heartbeat.

When she awoke, she felt the hard roof beneath her back. She stretched then opened her eyes to find that it was not the roof at all. Hannah sat up and saw the silver door before her. It was shining brighter than she'd ever seen it, as if it had been expecting her. She felt a sudden wave of courage and determination sweep over her.

"*You alone hold the key.*"

Jackson's voice rang through her head like a bell.

"*That's what you were born to do.*"

She marched to the door with determined steps and pulled the key from beneath her nightgown.

"*Whatever lies on the other side...*"

She put the key in the lock and turned it.

"*...is your destiny.*"

The door swung open and the room was flooded with a silver light. The princess shielded her eyes until it began to dissipate. When she looked up, she saw a figure standing there, silhouetted by the glow.

"Miss me?" came a deep voice.

Aedyn stepped out of the light, grinning. He ran to his sister and threw his arms around her, picking her up and spinning her around. The moment he touched her it was like a dam broke inside her head. A million thoughts and memories came rushing over all at once, spilling out from her eyes and splashing onto her brother's shirt.

He set her down, reaching up and brushing the tears from her cheek. Her heart was so full she thought it would burst. She let out a joyful laugh, like the tinkling of little bells, and flung her arms around him again. She squeezed him tightly, kicking up one heel behind her.

"Aedyn," she whispered, before stepping back again.

"First order of business: thanks for slamming the door in my face," he said.

"Aedyn, I'm so sorry! I'm so sorry, but I didn't—"

"—remember me?" he finished.

"Yes," she said, lowering her eyes as to not meet his gaze.

"I know. It's okay, Ember," Aedyn assured her, lifting her chin then taking her hands.

"But how...?"

"Well for starters I didn't actually think you would have screamed and shut the door on me if you'd known who I was," he laughed. "But more than that...well, it's really because of the door being there in the first place. We've always had a connection, you and I."

"It's a twin thing," Emberlynn smiled.

"It is," he said, smiling back, "but it's more than that. Here, let me show you something."

Aedyn let go of one of her hands and pulled her by the other toward the light.

"Can—can I go through there?"

"Don't worry, you'll be fine."

Hannah followed her brother through the door and found herself in another room identical to the one they'd just left.

"It's exactly the same, I know..." he said, noting the look of confusion on her face.

"What is this place?" Emberlynn asked.

"As far as I can tell, this room doesn't exist."

"But we're standing in it right now, having a conversation."

"Exactly. We are here right now."

"In a place that doesn't exist?"

"OK, how do I put this? It doesn't exist, not really, but it is real for us. We can get here, but only when you're—"

"—asleep," finished Emberlynn, beginning to understand. "So this room is in my mind?"

"No, this room is in my mind. That's why I was stuck on this side of the door. The other one is yours."

"So I'm inside your mind right now?"

"Sort of. But remember, this doesn't really exist. Does that make sense?"

"Well, yes and also no, not at all."

"Yeah, I know what you mean," he laughed.

"How is this possible?"

Emberlynn knew the answer before it was spoken.

"Magic."

"Magic," she repeated.

"Somehow we've created a place that only exists for us—a room in our minds and a door to each other. I've been reaching out for you and that is how my room is here. Subconsciously you must have been reaching back."

"I know I was. You've always been there, just below the surface. Something I was trying desperately to find, to remember. Something I could never quite reach."

Aedyn smiled at his sister.

"How did you know I'd forgotten you? You said it was because of the door?"

"I knew that if you remembered me I'd be able to get through that door. Somehow, I'd be able to reach you. I'd always been connected to you before. If something was wrong with you, I always knew, even if I wasn't with you. And you'd always known when I was hurt or in trouble. But suddenly I didn't feel you anymore. I felt completely alone. It was like I could feel you forgetting me. I knew you were on the other side but, try as I might, I couldn't open the door."

Emberlynn's lip quivered.

"It's not your fault, Ember. You created a place just for me without knowing it. You literally willed it into existence. That's pretty amazing."

"I don't feel amazing. I feel like the worst sister."

Tears began falling down her face.

"I'm so sorry, Aedyn. I don't know how I could ever have…" she trailed off. "No. I do. I do remember."

All of a sudden, an image began forming in her mind. She was in the garden of the palace of Gillodel in a pale pink dress. The fog that always surrounded her didn't seem as thick this time. She heard a voice behind her. Normally this sort of thing would frighten her, but this was a voice she'd heard a thousand times before in her dreams. It belonged to a boy that she'd never forgotten but couldn't quite remember. He was talking about Snowberries.

She turned around to look at him, but instead she saw a figure behind him through the fog. Dropping the fistful of Snowberries that had been in her hand, she put her finger to her lips and ducked behind a large rosebush. The boy followed.

A few moments later the shadow passed in front of them, followed closely by another. Emberlynn and the boy sat silently, barely breathing in the darkness. After a minute the princess peeked around the side of the bush and saw something she'd never seen before.

The shadows had made their way to the southern wall of the castle and, in that wall, they proceeded to open a door. It was mostly obscured by large vines growing up the side of the palace, but they squeezed through and Emberlynn held her breath.

"Come on," she whispered, when she'd had time to process what she was seeing.

"Ember, where are you going? Emberlynn!"

She darted from behind the bush, silently creeping toward the door. The boy followed begrudgingly. They made their way to another section of bushes closer to the palace and crouched down behind them just in time. The men had returned.

Through the fog Emberlynn could just make out two shapes coming out of the hidden door in the side of the palace. They seemed to be carrying something. They stepped into the starlight and she gasped quietly. Standing before her were Theron and Banning, and in their arms lay the unconscious body of her bother.

Emberlynn quickly formulated a plan: she would sneak away and get help—she would find her father and rescue her brother from a terrible fate—but this wasn't to be. She and the boy were fully concealed behind the small clump of bushes, but they'd failed to notice one crucial detail. As they tiptoed around the side of the rosebush they'd stepped in the pile of Snowberries, leaving a trail of luminous footprints behind them.

"Father," came Banning's voice from a few feet away. "Look."

He had seen the footprints and, by this time, so had the boy next to Emberlynn.

"Run!" he said to her, his voice quiet but urgent. "Run!"

He grabbed her hand and they fled through the garden toward the forest. But not before Theron saw them.

"Princess?!" he called after her. "Emberlynn! Come back!"

She did not.

"Bring them to me," he ordered his son. "I'll take care of the boy."

The princess ran as fast as her legs would carry her, hand in hand with the boy. While the rest of the memory had come back to her, somehow she could not focus on his face. Still she clung to his hand like her life depended on it. She heard Banning's voice calling after them.

"Emberlynn! Your Highness?"

Her legs were growing tired but the force of sheer panic carried her forward. She could see the Tarvys River glittering in the starlight. If she could just get across maybe she could hide in the forest. Without thinking Emberlynn dived into the river the moment she reached it, the boy at her heels. They emerged from the other side, dripping wet, and soldiered on.

It felt as if they'd been running forever and there seemed to be no end in sight. Everywhere they went they heard Banning's voice calling after them. They made a winding path through the forest, occasionally changing direction and weaving in and out of trees in the hope that this would make it more difficult to follow them.

Suddenly Emberlynn's dress caught on a root, forcing her to the ground with a *crash!* On the floor of the forest the princess started crying. She was cold and wet and covered in mud and moss. Something bad had just happened to her brother, and she was pretty sure something bad was about to happen to her.

"Come on, Ember, just a little further," the boy said, encouragingly.

"Where are we going?" she asked, through the tears.

"I don't know," he admitted. "Just a little bit further, and a little bit further after that, until we find a way out of this mess."

She tore herself free from the root and he helped her up. And then they ran. And ran and ran. Until Emberlynn ran straight into the arms of the man who had been chasing her. It was Theron. He had "finished with the boy," whatever that meant, and had come to tie off the loose ends.

"There you are, princess! We've been looking everywhere."

She tried to escape but he'd wrapped his arms forcefully around her.

"Calm down, princess. This will all be over in just a moment."

An icy wind rushed through the forest and overtook her. It was like the very blood in her veins had been frozen. The only warmth was that of the hand holding hers tightly, refusing to let go.

Theron put his hands on either side of her head and pressed her forehead to his, closing his eyes as he did so. Suddenly a fog began forming in her mind. It was as if whole pieces of her life were blurring until nothing remained of them. That nothingness was shoved back into a dark corner of her mind and locked away. And forgotten. Then she blacked out.

She opened her eyes and Aedyn was staring at her.

"Theron!" she said, angrily.

"What?"

"Theron," she repeated.

"I have no idea who that is."

Suddenly the princess realized that the day of the kidnapping, she hadn't either.

"Theron is—"

At that moment the light from the door began shining brighter. There was a sound like rushing wind and the princess found herself being pulled toward it.

"What's happening?!" she cried.

"You're waking up," Aedyn said, smiling sadly.

"But—"

"Don't worry, Ember. You can always find your way back."

She was sucked through the opening and the door shut with a *clang*, blowing out the candles on the chandelier and leaving her in the dark.

Moments later she woke on the rooftop surrounded by the golden-grey fog of first light and the soft, steady pounding of Jackson's heart. She was still lying in his arms.

The princess lay there for a moment, trying to process everything that had just happened. *Aedyn was alive.* Somehow, somewhere. Suddenly she was flooded with almost every emotion all at once. She was overjoyed at seeing her brother again, even if it wasn't real. Overjoyed at remembering him, but guilt-ridden at forgetting him at all. She was heartbroken at losing the past five years with him and furious at the same time. How could anyone be so cruel and heartless?

Banning. The full force of this finally hit her. *Banning!* Banning whom she had spent months with, whom she had fallen in love with, been engaged to! He and his father had kidnapped her brother and then come for her. It was too much to bear. She had known for some time that Banning was not who she'd first thought. She didn't love him anymore, but she had once. She had truly believed that he loved her, too, but it had all been a lie, a chess game.

And Aedyn—yes, he was alive. But where? And what could she do? If she went back to her old life and told her family what she now knew, would they believe her? After all, she had no proof. And she'd been gone for months. Would they think she'd gone mad? And how would she explain why she'd run away? Or how she knew Aedyn was still alive. She really would sound mad.

Theron and Banning would face justice; that much she knew—but not yet. First, she needed to find proof. She needed to find Aedyn. If only she knew how. The surge of hope she had felt at first began to die. She didn't even know where to begin. She was crushed beneath the weight of all this knowledge and uncertainty. She started sobbing.

"What? Why?" said Jackson, jolting awake at the sound of the girl crying in his arms.

"Hannah, are you okay? What's wrong?" he asked, sitting up and pulling her closer to him.

The only answer she could give him was more tears.

"Shhh. It's okay, it's okay" he whispered, pressing his chin into the top of her head. "Hannah."

More sobs.

"Hannah."

Quieter sobs.

"Emberlynn."

Silence.

The princess stopped crying, pulled away from him slowly, and looked questioningly into his eyes. Jackson reached up and wiped the last tear gently from her cheek. She expected to feel fear, panic. She waited for it to hit, but it never came. Instead she felt a peace wash over her as she searched those green eyes, their golden flecks dancing for her in the pale light.

"How long?" she asked. "How long have you known?"

Jackson didn't answer.

"You've known the whole time haven't you?"

He smiled sheepishly at her.

She wasn't sure how she would react until she heard herself laughing quietly.

"Why didn't you say anything?"

"You didn't want me to know," he said, simply. "It seemed like you just wanted a fresh start. I know what that's like. I think we all deserve a chance to be whoever we want to be. You wanted to be Hannah."

"Thank you," was all she could manage. She looked down, fidgeting with a ruffle on her nightdress.

After a minute she looked back at Jackson and added, "You're my best friend, you know. You and Kinleigh. I'm sorry I lied to you. I almost told you a hundred times. It's just...no one has ever given me the chance to just be Emberlynn. Everyone expects me to be *Her Royal Highness the Great and Proper Princess of Ardia*, but I've never really fit that mold."

"You can be Emberlynn or Hannah or Empress of the mermaids. You're still my best friend."

Hannah smiled.

"Do the others know?"

"No. No, I don't think so."

"How did you figure it out?"

"Well, you don't exactly act like a commoner."

Emberlynn laughed.

"Can I ask you something?"

"Sure."

"Why were you crying?"

Her face fell. For a moment she had forgotten the daunting task she now faced.

"It's my brother," she said, finally.

"So you've remembered, then?"

Her face asked the question she couldn't put into words.

"Everyone in the two kingdoms knows that after Prince Aedyn disappeared, Princess Emberlynn didn't remember him or any of the events surrounding his disappearance. But no one knows why."

"I do."

The princess told him about her dreams and visions. She told him they'd been getting clearer and that last night she'd finally seen the whole picture—Theron, Banning, the memory charm...

Jackson stared at her in pensive silence, taking everything in.

"And Jackson..."

"Yeah?"

"Aedyn is alive."

CHAPTER 19

ONCOMING STORM

Jackson helped Emberlynn down from the roof and they crept quietly inside the house. Everyone else was still in bed. By the time she had washed and dressed, Charlotte was putting breakfast on the table.

It was one of the longest days in Emberlynn's memory. Shops were open again and they were back at work. Emberlynn, however, had a hard time concentrating and she absentmindedly pricked a few unsuspecting customers with a pin as she fitted them. After the third incident, Charlotte set her to work on some bookkeeping, saying it was probably best they leave the fittings to Kinleigh for the remainder of the day.

An hour before closing time they heard the ding of the bell tied to the front door of the shop.

"Be with you in a moment!" Charlotte called from the back room.

"Hi, Mom!" came Jackson's voice.

"Oh, hey. Come in."

"Actually I was hoping I could talk to Hannah."

Emberlynn poked her head out of the other room. She started to speak but lost her words when she saw Jackson. He had come straight from working the fields with Cavan and was still wearing his work clothes. His hair was tousled, his face flushed, and his skin beginning to freckle from the sun. There was a bit of dirt across his cheek.

Emberlynn stared at him for a moment, her pulse quickening as her mind went blank.

"What's up?" she said, finally, snapping herself out of the momentary daze.

"I have a few... ummm...errands I need to run before the shops close. I was hoping you might come along and help me out."

"That's really up to your mother."

"Sure, sweetie," said Charlotte. "We're pretty much done for the day."

"Ooo, can I come?!" asked Kinleigh, popping into the room.

Jackson shot her a look of warning through disapproving eyes.

"On second thought, I actually have a few things I need to finish up here."

"Okay, we'll see you at home in a bit," said Jackson, nodding to his sister.

"What was that about?" asked Charlotte, after they'd left.

"I have no idea."

∾

"Where are we going?" Emberlynn asked, when they were outside the shop.

Jackson headed down the street, the princess at his heels.

"I can't stop thinking about what you told me this morning, about Aedyn."

"Me either," she said quietly.

"What are you going to do?"

"Honestly, I have no idea. I don't even know where to start."

"I generally find that when I've lost something the best place to start is by retracing my steps."

She looked at him questioningly, unsure of his meaning.

"I think I might be able to help."

By this point in the conversation the pair had reached the town bookshop. Emberlynn followed Jackson inside.

"Hello Jackson. Miss Hannah," Tilford greeted them. "What brings you two in this evening?"

"We just returned yesterday from the ball at Gillodel," answered Jackson.

"You and half the kingdom," the bookkeeper laughed.

"Indeed. Well, Hannah had never been to Gillodel and she was really quite taken with it. She was hoping to learn more about it, and I thought maybe you'd have some books she could read."

"I certainly do. Back wall, on the left. Near where you found that architecture book for Cavan, Hannah."

"Thanks, Tilford," said Emberlynn, cheerily.

They headed to the back of the shop.

"What are we looking for?" Emberlynn whispered.

"Let's see..." Jackson mused. "*Ages of Lemeth, Rise and Fall of the Dark Days, An Ornithological Study of Lemeth*...No, no, and absolutely not. Ah, here we go. *Gillodel, Past and Present.*"

He pulled the book from the shelf and sat cross-legged on the floor. Emberlynn joined him, looking confused. Jackson opened to the back of the book, where he found a large map of the city.

"Let's do a math problem."

Emberlynn crinkled her nose disapprovingly at this suggestion.

"Using the facts you told me from your dream."

This sparked her interest a little.

"Theron is an evil, kidnapping memory wiper. He needs to hide a body weighing somewhere around 100 lbs. Let's say he has roughly fifteen minutes to hide the body and return before someone notices, and before he has to go chase a thirteen-year-old girl through the woods."

"I don't like this math problem."

"Stay with me. If these are the facts, then what is the maximum distance from the point of kidnapping that Theron could go to hide the body before having to turn around?"

Emberlynn's heart stopped.

"Oh my gosh," she said. "Jackson, you're a genius!"

"I have my moments," he grinned.

"Aedyn has to be somewhere in Gillodel, near the palace. There's no way Theron could have gone, what, more than half a mile before he had to come back?"

"Exactly."

Jackson leaned over the map and put his finger firmly on the palace, tracing a circle around it with his other hand.

"So he must be somewhere in this circle."

As he leaned over, the chain around his neck fell from beneath his shirt.

"What's that?" Emberlynn asked, pointing to the dainty silver star pendant hanging from the chain.

"Nothing," he said, tucking it quickly back inside his shirt.

"I thought we were past secrets," she whined.

"It belonged to someone I used to know a long time ago—someone that I lost," he said, looking at the floor.

"Oh. I'm sorry, Jackson."

"Life goes on," he said, looking up at her with a sad smile. "Now, if we're going to find the someone that you lost, we need to focus."

"Jackson..." Hannah said, suddenly, as something caught the corner of her eye. "Do you believe in magical families?"

He froze and looked at her warily.

"What do you mean?"

She stood up and looked over her shoulder, making sure Tilford wasn't looking. Then she pulled a book bound in red leather from the very back of the top shelf. It glowed slightly as she opened it to a page near the middle and handed it to him.

"*Magical Families: Fact or Fiction?*" he read, quietly.

"I found this when I was in buying Cavan's present, and wasn't sure what to make of it."

Jackson finished the page and continued on to the next few that followed it.

"Obviously Theron has some sort of magic. Fairy godmothers have been out of service for years and magic seemed to have dried up. The only thing that makes sense is that Theron and Banning are from a magical family."

"Yes. I think that's probably true."

"Jackson?" she whispered.

He leaned in closer.

"How can Aedyn and I see each other? Clearly, it's magic of some sort. I was wondering..." she trailed off.

"What were you wondering?"

"We're descendants of Cinderella. Does that mean we have magic, too?"

Jackson sat silent for a bit, thinking it over. Then he nodded toward the book.

"As you know fairy magic isn't all that powerful. Fairy godmothers can accomplish a lot with that magic, but it doesn't really leave much of a trace. You probably have a little magic in your veins, both of you. And that's part of the reason you can reach each other. It sounds to me like you both have a touch of mind-centric magic."

"Part of the reason?"

"If you ask me, it sounds like fairy dust is involved—obviously the door was cast with it."

He paused for a moment, choosing his next words carefully.

"Maybe this door isn't entirely in your mind after all."

"What do you mean?"

"You don't have any fairy dust do you?"

"No. I actually think I might be allergic to it."

"Well if you don't have any fairy dust, and Aedyn doesn't have any either—I'm assuming he doesn't—then there would be no way for you to use it to create a portal between you. Emberlynn..." he breathed in the smallest whisper. "What if the door exists both in your mind and somewhere in the real world?"

They stared at each other for a few minutes, thinking about the implications of this idea. Then Jackson glanced out the window.

"Oh gosh, the sun's nearly set. We should head home before my parents start to worry."

Jackson stood quickly and Emberlynn followed suit. He placed *Gillodel, Past and Present* back on the shelf. But *Magic and Myth* he clutched tightly in his hand. Emberlynn didn't notice.

As they walked past the counter, she said goodbye to Tilford and went outside. Jackson lingered behind for a moment. He held the book up with a serious expression. Tilford nodded at him, and he placed the book under his shirt before joining Emberlynn outside.

They walked home swiftly and silently. When they reached the door of the cottage, Jackson stopped. He had been watching determination grow on Emberlynn's face the entire walk home.

"You're going after him, aren't you?"

She nodded.

"If Aedyn is in Gillodel, then that's where I need to be."

"How are you going to find him?"

"I don't know. But if I don't try then I never will."

She reached for the door and he grabbed her gently by the arm.

"At least wait a few days. Promise me that. Take some time to think it through and come up with some sort of plan. I'll help you."

Emberlynn nodded.

"A few days," she agreed, opening the door and walking inside.

⧼⧽

Back at Whitehawk, Theron and Banning were also formulating a plan.

"It's quite simple," Theron was saying.

"We stay here until after the prince's wedding. King Edric and Queen Gwyneria will be in attendance. You return to Ardia with them after the ceremony, saying how painful it was for you to be reminded that your own wedding to Emberlynn may never happen. Tell them this has renewed your fervor to find her and ask permission to head up another kingdom-wide search for her. After a few more months they'll give up the search and the king will have to select a new heir. Being the broken-hearted fiancé of their beloved daughter, you will be the natural choice."

"And how long do I have to be the broken-hearted fiancé?"

"Just until Edric names you as his heir. Then you can do whatever you like. His first act upon doing so will probably be to find you a bride. And you shall have your pick of any beauty in the three kingdoms."

"It's a pity Emberlynn disappeared," sighed Banning. "She would have made this whole process so much easier. And I must say it will be difficult to find another as beautiful as she."

"True enough."

There was a knock at the door. They heard voices outside as their servant came into the dining hall.

"A messenger from the palace, Your Grace."

"Send him in."

A tall gangly man entered the room.

"The king has just gotten word from Tardyn that Princess Sierra is on her way back to Lemeth," he said. "She should be here in a few days, and the wedding ceremony will be held one week from Saturday."

He handed the duke a parchment bearing the royal seal.

"They hope you will be in attendance."

"Please tell His Highness we will be delighted to attend."

The messenger bowed and returned to the palace.

"Excellent," said Theron, once he was gone. "Let the games begin."

⁓

Sleep did not come easily to Emberlynn that night. She was anxious to see Aedyn again and her mind raced with things she wanted to tell him and questions she wanted to ask. She tossed and turned for an hour or so, but finally found herself once again on a cold marble floor in the dark.

She snapped her fingers and the chandelier blazed to life. There, standing in the open doorway, was Aedyn. Emberlynn grinned.

"We have a lot to talk about," she said, walking through the portal.

Emberlynn sat down on the floor against the wall, a few feet down from the door. She motioned for her brother to join her.

"Then we had better get started," he replied, sitting down beside her. "You can start by telling me who Theron is."

So she did. She started at the beginning, telling him how she had met Banning and all about their engagement. She walked him through her running away, sneaking onto Ben's cart, meeting Jackson, the ball, Damian's engagement...everything. Finally she told him about the memories flooding back to her of the kidnapping and Theron's memory charm.

"Woah," he said, after she had told him everything. "Sounds like I've missed a lot. The last thing I remember was the ball for Damian's sixteenth birthday. How old is he now?"

"Twenty-one," she said, quietly.

"Wait, are we eighteen now?"

"Yes."

"I guess it seems odd that I don't know that," he said. "Time passes very strangely here, wherever here is. I get older, but I have no way of marking the passing of days. I don't get hungry or thirsty and I never sleep. I just sort of...exist."

"That's awful!"

"I suppose, but it could be worse. Time goes by quickly. If I'd had to guess I would have said I'd been here maybe a year. I'd never imagined it was..." he trailed off.

"Five years is a long time," said Emberlynn.

"How was your eighteenth birthday ball? Was is as amazing as I always pictured?"

"Sort of. I mean, that was the night of the engagement and... well I ran away the next day."

"Right, you mentioned that."

"The last thing I remember," he continued, after a pause, "is leaving the throne room at Gillodel looking for you and Aaver. Then—"

"Wait, who's Aaver?"

Aedyn stared at her, a puzzled expression on his face.

"I'm pretty sure he's the boy who was with you when I was taken. I thought you knew that."

"No. I've never known who the boy was."

"The three of us used to play together when we'd visit Gillodel in the summers. He was one of our best friends. His father was the Duke of Kingston."

"But Theron is Duke of Kingston."

There was a moment of stunned silence between them.

"Aedyn, one of Uncle Thomas' friends was blamed for your kidnapping. I think it was Aaver's father."

"What happened to them?"

"They were exiled. Jackson said there was no real proof."

"That's because he didn't do it!" he shouted, pounding the floor with his fist.

Emberlynn scooted closer to her brother, putting her head on his shoulder.

"It was terrible," said Aedyn quietly, after a few minutes of silence.

"What was?"

"That night. I left the ball because I couldn't find you or Aaver. I had just stepped into the corridor when something grabbed my leg. I looked down and..."

He paused for a moment and his sister felt a shudder run through his body.

"Some...thing was coming up out of the tapestry on the floor—some creature made of thread. It pulled me into the floor somehow. Next thing I knew I was popping up in the library on top of another great rug. It was terrible magic."

He shuddered again.

"And there were the people I now know to be Theron and Banning. They knocked me unconscious by blowing some sort of powder in my face. I woke up here."

"Do you have any clues as to where 'here' might be?"

"All I know is that it looks exactly like this room, but when you're not here the door is gone."

"So you're in a white marble room?"

"I'm not so sure I'm anywhere."

"How is that possible?"

"I seem to be in a place between places. Somewhere only magic can reach."

"That somewhere is in Gillodel—at least the entrance is."

Emberlynn explained to him what Jackson had told her just a few hours before.

"Ohhh no, Ember. No. I know that look. You are not going to Gillodel," he said, firmly.

"It's the only way! There must be a way to reach you. If only I can find it."

"Ember, it isn't safe! If Theron is there what's to stop him from erasing your memory again?"

"I'll be careful, I promise!"

"Are you happy in Faryn?" he asked. "As Hannah?"

"Yes."

"Then stay there. I'm begging you. You're safe there. It sounds like this Jackson fellow will look after you."

"That's ridiculous, Aed!" Emberlynn argued. "I refuse to sit back and do nothing while you're locked away in a state of quasi-existence! Not now that I know."

"Ember—"

"I will find you!" she said, every ounce of determination she had showing on her stone-cold face.

Before Aedyn realized what was happening, his sister had darted through the portal, slamming the door and locking it behind her.

Bang. Bang.

"Don't do this, Ember!" begged a voice from the other side.

She snapped her fingers again, extinguishing the lights in the room. She closed her eyes, and when she opened them again, she was lying in her bed with the sun peeking through the window. Taking a deep breath she sat up, wrapping her arms around herself.

"I guess there's nothing for it," Emberlynn whispered finally, swinging her feet to the floor.

Not bothering to wash or dress, Emberlynn opened her bedroom door and walked decidedly into the kitchen. Charlotte was frying some ham in the skillet and Cavan was sitting at the table with his nose in a book.

"I have to go away for a bit," she blurted out.

They both looked up at her curiously.

"I've just received news that there's a family matter I must attend to."

"Of course, dear," Charlotte replied softly. "I do hope everything's alright."

Emberlynn looked at the floor.

"When will you be leaving?" asked Cavan.

"Three days," Jackson said firmly, walking into the kitchen. She shot him a dirty look.

"She told me so yesterday," he added. "And I told her she really should take these days off work to prepare for her journey. There's so much she needs to get done, but she wouldn't hear it."

"Oh, Hannah, of course you must. If you have things to tend to, I insist you do so."

"How long will you be away?" Cavan asked.

"I wish I knew. As long as it takes to sort things out. But I'll return as soon as I'm able."

"Well you'll certainly be missed."

She smiled at him.

"I suppose I should get dressed now," she said, finally taking note of her disheveled appearance and feeling suddenly sheepish.

She scurried off to her room. As soon as she was gone Jackson noticed Cavan was frowning and muttering something into his teacup.

"I'm going to stay in and help her," said Jackson quietly, sitting down in the chair beside his father.

"What's going on, Son?"

Jackson shook his head.

"My concern has been growing for some time now. Something isn't right. I can feel it, like a storm brewing in my veins."

"Do you trust me, Father?"

Cavan studied his son's face for a moment then nodded.

"There is a storm coming. And Hannah needs me, or..."

"Or?"

"Or I'm not sure she'll be able to weather it."

Cavan clasped his son by the shoulder.

"I wish you'd tell me what you know, but it seems you aren't going to. Just look after her, Son. We've grown quite fond of her."

"So have I."

Cavan gave his son a knowing smile.

CHAPTER 20

UNMASKED

By the time Emberlynn came back into the kitchen, everyone but Jackson was gone. He was sitting at the table sipping a cup of tea.

"They've all left already, then?"

Jackson nodded.

"Kinleigh got up just after you went to get ready. She scarfed down breakfast and they all headed out to work."

Emberlynn sat down in front of the plate of food Charlotte had left for her.

"You know I wanted to leave this morning," she said.

"Yes, but you promised not to," he replied.

"I suppose I did," she said, laughing. "Why aren't you in the field with Cavan?"

"He's letting me stay in and help you."

"You didn't—"

"Don't worry, I didn't tell him," he said, chuckling. "But you can't just go trekking off without a plan. So hurry up and eat your breakfast and let's get going."

"And where exactly are we going?" she asked, between bites of toast.

Jackson crossed his arms and stared at her.

"Alright, alright!" she laughed, quickly finishing the rest of her food.

A few minutes later they were standing in the middle of the large grove of trees on the edge of their land.

"What are we doing here?"

In reply, Jackson picked up a long slender branch from the ground and snapped it in half. He handed one half to Emberlynn and grinned.

She raised an eyebrow at him in question.

"You have no idea what you will encounter in Gillodel."

"And you do?"

"Not at all. That's just the point. You have to be prepared for anything."

Jackson stepped forward with his right foot, bent his knees slightly, and extended the branch in his hand toward Emberlynn. A light of understanding flickered in her eyes, and she did the same.

"Ready?" he asked.

She nodded, lunging forward. Before she knew what was happening Jackson had parried her attack, knocking her branch to the ground. He picked it up and handed it to her again.

"I don't know how to do this," she admitted sheepishly, taking the branch.

"Which is exactly why we are doing it. Again..."

Jackson spent the next two hours teaching the princess to defend herself. He showed her the proper stance, the best way to hold a weapon, and a few basic attacks and parries. She was getting blisters on her hand when he finally dropped his branch saying,

"Let's call it a day. Not bad for your first lesson."

"Where did you learn all this?"

"I've done some traveling," he said, matter-of-factly. "You pick things up."

From there the pair trudged down to the lake to cool off. As soon as they got there Emberlynn dived in headfirst. As she came up out of the water, she noticed a muddy brown liquid dripping from her hair; she had forgotten that she'd colored it for the ball. She spent the next several minutes scrubbing her hair in the water, while Jackson splashed around her, laughing.

"I'll never understand the things girls do when they get dolled up."

"Well I wasn't about to walk into my uncle's palace as a blonde, now was I? He and Damian would have recognized me instantly, even with the mask. Let alone Banning."

She shuddered every time she said that name.

"Fair point."

By this time the water was running clear and her hair was a shining shade of blonde again.

"That's not going to kill the fish or anything, is it?"

"No," she replied, laughing. "It's mostly just clay that Kinleigh and I dug up from the shore here—that mixed with a few spices. It's perfectly safe."

She swam over to Jackson and patted him patronizingly on the head. He stuck his tongue out at her.

They splashed around for a little longer then headed back to the cottage.

"Now it really is time we sit down and work out a proper plan," said Jackson, once they were inside.

"Actually, would you mind going to Charlotte's shop and picking up a few things for me?"

She found a bit of parchment and jotted down a list for him.

"Why do you need all this?" he questioned.

She shot him a look of warning.

"Yeah, alright," he agreed. "What are you going to do?"

"I'm going back to the book shop to get that book on Gillodel. I need to get a better feel for the city."

"Not a bad idea. Ok, I'll grab this stuff from my mother and meet you back here in a bit. We can go over that book."

They dried off and got changed before heading into town.

∾

Emberlynn heard the familiar clink of the bell as she walked into the bookshop.

"Hello, Hannah. What can I help you with?"

"Hi, Tilford," she replied cheerfully. "I was hoping to buy a book I saw here earlier."

Tilford reached down beneath the counter. He smiled at her and brought forth a book.

She looked down at it.

"*Gillodel, Past and Present.* But, how...?"

He grinned mysteriously but said only, "I visited Gillodel once, a few years ago. It's a beautiful place."

Emberlynn nodded and reached into her pocket to pay for the book.

"It's a gift," Tilford said.

"I couldn't possibly—"

"I insist."

"Thank you. I guess I'll be off then. I'm supposed to meet Jackson."

He nodded.

"Hannah," he called, as she turned to leave. "Be careful."

She looked at him questioningly. He touched the side of his nose with one finger in reply.

"I will," she promised.

Then she headed back to the cottage.

⁂

When she walked inside Jackson was sitting at the table behind a heap of fabric.

"Are you going to tell me what all this is for?"

"I need to sew myself a cloak. I can't exactly march into the city with no cover in broad daylight."

Jackson nodded approvingly.

"Then why don't you start on that and I'll find useful bits of information from that book and read them to you?"

Emberlynn handed him the book. He nosed through it while she surveyed the pile of fabric. She selected a thick deep green cloth and began cutting pieces.

"Gillodel is a small city located just north of the Tavys River," Jackson read. "It is the capital city of the kingdom of Lemeth and is best known for being home to Snow White."

"Yes, I know all that."

"Yeah, I don't think we'll learn much from the history chapters. Maybe people or geography?" he said, flipping ahead.

Emberlynn made fair progress on her cloak while Jackson called out facts about the areas surrounding the palace and the people who live there. They didn't find anything particularly earth shattering, but it was helpful for her to learn the lay of the land.

By the time the others returned home that evening Emberlynn had stashed the fabric and book away in her room, and had dinner waiting.

"Hannah!" Charlotte cried. "You didn't have to make dinner."

"Really it's the least I can do."

"Well thank you, dear. It looks delicious."

Emberlynn was fairly certain it wouldn't be. She hadn't done much cooking in her time, but it had actually turned out quite well. She was pleased. She must have picked up more than she knew from watching Charlotte work in the kitchen.

After dinner she retreated to her room for the night. She could easily finish her cloak tomorrow, but she had another project to get started on tonight. Her plan was to sew herself a new dress: simple, but elegant. If she was going to walk into the palace and reveal herself as royalty, she was going to look the part. Picking up the other fabric Jackson had brought her, she turned it over in her hands. It was the deepest shade of midnight blue with little bits that glinted as they caught the candlelight. She grabbed her scissors, needle, and thread, and got to work. She hadn't been at it long when she heard a familiar soft thump above her head.

"That'll be Jackson," she thought, with a sad smile.

Part of her wanted to join him on the roof; she was pretty sure he was waiting for her. But she knew she couldn't. For starters she had a lot of work to do on the dress and not much time in which to do it. It was crucial that Jackson didn't find out about it. She couldn't tell him she planned to reveal herself—he would never allow it. She also knew it was her best chance at finding her brother. It would allow her free roam of the palace and surrounding areas, and it would also give her access to Theron and Banning. If she played her cards right, she might be able to glean some information from them.

But it was more than that. Emberlynn knew she needed to start distancing herself from Jackson. They had grown quite close over the past four months.

"Four months," she said aloud.

It was hard to believe it had been that long, but she had left at the beginning of May and it was just a few days shy of September. In that time Jackson had become her best friend. She would be lying to herself if she said there weren't other feelings growing inside her, threatening to overwhelm friendship, but she also knew that wasn't an option. Jackson was amazing and maybe in another life, if she hadn't been Princess of Ardia and they'd just met one day under different circumstances. But she was Princess of Ardia and she was in love with Aaver. Putting a name to the voice echoing through her mind had somehow made it more real. She loved him and she knew, in the deepest part of her heart, that she could never love another—not while he walked the earth.

That was the other reason she was going to the palace: she hoped she might be able to find some information about his whereabouts. His family had been exiled, yes, but surely they kept some sort of record of where they'd gone. Emberlynn walked to the window and stared up at the sky. Jackson was looking up at the same stars. Maybe, somewhere, Aaver was, too. She sighed sadly, then sat back down upon her bed. She had work to do.

The next two days flew by. Emberlynn finished her cloak the first day, as well as the book on Gillodel. They also had a few more fencing lessons, this time with real swords.

"Where on earth did you get these?" Emberlynn asked him, admiring the sword in her hand. "These are really well made."

"I thought you didn't know how to fence?"

"I may not know how to use a sword," she said, "but I've been around them my whole life. I am a princess, after all."

"That you are, Your Highness," he said, grinning as he bowed to her.

"Oh shut up!" she said, laughing.

"Make me," he challenged with a smirk.

Emberlynn took up an attack stance and they got back to work.

After two mostly sleepless nights, Emberlynn had also managed to finish her dress. It was a high waisted column dress that fell just above the ground. It was, admittedly, a bit more form fitting than was customary, but, after all, she was looking to make an entrance. She got up before dawn on the third day, put on her dress and cloak, and tiptoed silently out of the cottage. She was terrible at goodbyes and decided it was probably better to avoid this one altogether. She took one last look at the cottage then turned southward toward Gillodel.

It was a long uneventful day. She brought enough money to buy lunch in a village she passed along the way. Other than that, she stopped only twice to rest. She met hardly anyone on the road, made good time, and passed unnoticed and unrecognized. But she couldn't shake the feeling she was being watched.

"I wonder if Aedyn can see me," she mused. *"I hope he's not too cross with me."*

She reached Gillodel just as the sun began to set. The sky fire lit up the crowds of people who were buzzing around the palace in preparation for Damian's wedding. It was just four days away. When she arrived at the palace, she saw Damian sitting on the steps out front, gazing up at the sky. There were people walking past him in all directions but he gave no notice; he was deep in thought. She approached him slowly with small, determined steps.

"Who goes there?!" came a menacing voice.

One of the guards had walked through the palace door and noticed a small, cloaked figure making their way toward the prince. Emberlynn kept walking, paying him no heed, but the commotion had jolted Damian from his thoughts and he was eyeing her warily.

"Halt in the name of the King!" called the guard again.

Emberlynn stopped walking and threw her hood back off her face.

"Can't a girl congratulate her cousin on his engagement without the whole kingdom going up in arms?" she asked coyly, now throwing her cloak off entirely.

As she did so the setting sun caught her dress, refracting into a million tiny pieces of light and making her, too, appear as the night sky set on fire. Her hair, which had now grown past her shoulders, fell in a gentle curl. Everyone fell silent as she stood there, as a star that had fallen to the earth.

"Emberlynn?!" Damian cried, springing up and running to her.

He threw his arms around her in a tender embrace. Then a loud cry went up from the crowd.

"It's Emberlynn! It's the lost princess!"

"Beg pardon, Your Highness," said the guard sheepishly, bowing.

The princess nodded and offered a forgiving smile.

"You did not know."

People were pressing in now and had formed a circle around the princess and her cousin.

"What's all this commotion about?" shouted King Thomas, as he and his wife descended the steps of the palace. "We've got a wedding to plan for, and..." he trailed off. "Emberlynn? Emberlynn!" he cried as he rushed forward through the crowd.

"You!" he ordered, pointing to the guardsman. "Send word to Edric and Gwyneria immediately. Their daughter has returned!"

"Yes, Your Majesty!" said the man, bowing. "Right away!"

"Now...silence!" demanded the king, once the guard had run off with the message.

The crowd obeyed instantly.

"Emberlynn," he said, stepping forward. "Dear Emberlynn." He hugged her tightly. "Where have you been?"

And just like that all her best laid plans fell apart.

"I...I..." she stammered.

By this time the news of Emberlynn's return had spread through the whole palace.

"Emberlynn!" came a clear, cold voice.

She took a deep breath then turned around.

"Banning."

"Dearest Emberlynn."

He ran into the circle of people and pulled her close to him. "Wherever have you been, my love?"

She patted him gently on the back before pulling away.

"We were just asking the same thing," said Queen Alette.

Theron joined them as she was speaking. He stood silently on the edge of the circle with a somber expression as he took everything in.

Emberlynn froze. She couldn't tell them why she had left. Wasn't that the whole point? But somehow in the fire of her determination to find her brother, all logic and reason had faded away. Hadn't that been the very reason she had hidden her plans from Jackson? He was far too logical to miss a crucial detail like this one. She wished now that she had told him. He would have reminded her why she couldn't come here, why she couldn't do exactly what she'd just done. And he probably would have had a better idea. She wished now that he was here.

"He would know what to do," she thought. *"But he's not here. And what, by Cinderella's slipper, do I tell them?"*

"I..." she began again. "I—"

"She was with me!" she heard a familiar voice say.

"Isn't that odd?" the princess thought. "I miss Jackson so terribly much that I'm hearing his voice in my head."

I wasn't until she saw him step through the crowd into the circle of people that she realized it wasn't in her head at all. She stared at him, complete and total shock evident on her face.

"Seize him!" King Thomas cried, angrily.

Three guards rushed through the crowd and grabbed Jackson. Emberlynn was too stunned to speak.

"I would have thought you'd know better than to come here, old friend," Damian snarled, spitting out the last two words like a poison. "But it seems you haven't quite grasped the meaning of the term exile."

"What—" Emberlynn began.

"She was kidnapped!" interrupted Theron. "Kidnapped by the son of the very man who took her brother all those years ago!"

Theron, it seemed, was a master of theatrics and he was putting on quite a show.

"How brave of you to have escaped, Highness," he said. "And how very foolish of you to follow!" he added, turning to Jackson.

Emberlynn couldn't move; couldn't breathe.

"W-what...?"

"And the poor dear...didn't even know."

He wove his words together like a net, carefully laying a trap for his listeners. No one would ever doubt Theron, Duke of Whitehawk.

"Take him to the dungeon," said Thomas quietly, pain evident in his deep brown eyes. "We'll deal with him after the wedding. For now let us celebrate the return of my niece and the marriage of my son."

With that he turned and walked back inside the palace.

CHAPTER 21

A PROMISE KEPT

Jackson did not struggle as the guards marched him away, but Emberlynn ran toward him.

"Wait!" she demanded.

The guards halted but kept their grip on Jackson.

"What are they talking about, Jackson?" she whispered.

"You've got a way in now, Emmie. Theron will have figured out what's going on, so be careful. But your uncle is satisfied with this explanation. Everyone else will be, too."

"We've got to lock him up now, Highness," said one of the guards.

They dragged him back from her but this time he put up a fight. He lunged forward, grabbing Emberlynn. He pulled her to him and kissed her. It was as if the world kept turning but Emberlynn did not. Everything spun around her and she saw a hundred moments in her mind, suddenly snapped into perfect clarity. Jackson's face was in all of them.

He was there on the beach, calling to her to join him and Aedyn in the water. But her father wouldn't let her. He was there in the great hall as Gwyneria scolded her for fidgeting at the table. And he was there with her in the garden, watching her brother's kidnapping, never letting go of her hand.

She also saw countless little moments that no one else had ever seen; him squeezing her hand when no one was looking, a wink from across the room, stealing a kiss behind a pillar in a deserted corridor... This was the boy she had fallen in love with, and nobody else had known.

In a moment the visions were gone and she was standing in front of the palace steps with his lips pressed against hers.

The guards pulled him back and one of them struck him across the cheek. Tears streamed down the princess' face and her lip quivered.

"Aaver?" she whispered as they hurried him away.

"Told you I'd never forget," he winked. "Now find our boy, Emmie!"

There was sadness in his eyes as he disappeared from view, but there was a light of courage shining through. He had sacrificed himself to give her a chance to find her brother and she was determined not to let him down.

⁓

The rest of the evening had been a blur. Emberlynn's aunt had ushered her into the palace, where her family fawned over her. After she had been force-fed the most elaborate supper she'd had in months, she was finally taken to the guest wing. She had requested that no one but family be permitted to see her that evening; a request which her uncle granted, keeping even Banning and Theron away. This, admittedly, was her primary reason for asking. Fortunately her uncle had also issued a decree that she was not to be bothered with questions because she had been through a traumatic experience and wasn't to be

194

made to talk about it. This freed her from having to explain herself further.

Once upstairs her aunt drew a hot bath for her and left her alone with her thoughts. Guards were posted at every entrance and she had requested all rugs and tapestries be removed from the entire guest wing of the palace. She was, at least for now, out of Theron's reach. She bathed quickly, curled up in bed, and faded into a dreamless sleep. There were so many thoughts spinning frantically in her head that her mind had simply shut down.

She awoke the next morning to find fresh clothes at the foot of her bed and a tray of breakfast on her bedside table. The princess sat in bed, looking around the room. With her memories back she now recalled that this was the room where she had always stayed on their visits to Lemeth. It had a south-facing window that overlooked the gardens. She climbed out of bed and went to the window seat, grabbing a biscuit and some jam from the tray as she passed. As she thoughtfully munched her biscuit, she surveyed the garden below. It was impossible for her not to replay that night in her mind. She could see it all—where they carried Aedyn across the garden, where she and Aaver had hidden, the spot where the garden met the river, and the forest beyond.

"I need to get a better view," she thought.

She dressed quickly then opened the door to her room, peeking her head out.

"I want to see my fiancé!" came an irritated voice from down the hall.

Emberlynn closed the door quietly then pressed her ear against it and listened.

"I'm sorry, sir," answered a second voice.

It sounded vaguely familiar. Emberlynn thought it was guard who had stopped her the night before.

"But the king says no one is to disturb her. Needs her rest, she does. She's been through an ordeal."

"It's afternoon already! Surely she's awake by now."

"I have my orders."

"If your orders are to not wake her, then wouldn't they be irrelevant it she was already awake?"

"I suppose so."

"Well, can you check?"

The princess darted back to her bed and burrowed under the covers. She had just laid her head on the pillow when she heard the door creak open. She heard footsteps and felt someone standing over her, but she kept her eyes tightly closed. After a moment the footsteps retreated and the door closed.

"Still asleep," came the guard's voice.

Banning let out an exasperated sigh.

"Well can you let me know when she isn't?"

"Yes sir."

Banning's footsteps faded down the hallway and Emberlynn crawled silently out of bed again. She walked out of her room and was greeted by the guard.

"Morning, Your Highness," he said with a bow.

"Good morning. What's your name?"

"Charlie, Your Highness."

"Call me Emberlynn, please!"

"I'd rather not, Miss, if it's all the same to you."

"Alright. Well do me a favor, then," she said, heading down the corridor. "If he comes back 'round again, tell him I'm still asleep, yeah?"

"Of course, Your Highness."

She hadn't had a title in such a long time that it seemed quite silly now—all the bowing and the pomp and circumstance. Being a royal did have its perks, though. After all, everyone had to do what she said, which would make the search for her brother that much easier. All the same, she planned to keep her search a secret. She had revealed too much the previous night, and it had cost her Jackson...Aaver. Strange.

She was still trying to wrap her head around it. The love of her life had been living under the same roof for four months and she hadn't recognized him. But then again, her twin brother had been missing for five years and she hadn't even remembered he existed. At least she had remembered Aaver, even if she had no idea who he was.

"Does that make me a horrible sister? Probably."

But of course she couldn't control what Theron erased from her mind. And then a thought occurred to her.

"I wonder...surely Theron had, in fact, intended to erase those pieces entirely from my mind. But then why was I able to remember? He was able to lock them away. But they were never completely gone."

The princess had enough to worry about at the moment, however, and she soon dismissed this thought from her mind.

"Clearly he wasn't as powerful as he thought."

And that was that.

Emberlynn was on a mission. She tiptoed through the guest wing to the other side of the palace, managing to remain unseen. Being the princess, she was allowed to go wherever she pleased, but she didn't feel like explaining why she wanted to go there. It involved ducking behind a few statues and suits of armor, but she made it there without any questions.

There before her was a large wooden door. She pushed it open quietly, closing it behind her. There was nothing in the small room, save a giant spiral staircase leading upward and disappearing into the heights of the castle—the entrance to the tower.

The princess climbed the staircase slowly, having to stop once for a moment to catch her breath. When she reached the top, she walked through another door then ran to the window, looking down at the grounds below. She could still only see southward. The garden beneath her was dotted with specs of color (flowers just reaching their full bloom), and the large silver fountain glittered in the sun. She wasn't getting anywhere looking south—she needed a full 360-degree view. So she walked over and took hold of the ladder in the middle of the room. She climbed it, reaching a small trapdoor in the roof and pushing it open. The sun streamed in as she squeezed through the door and climbed out onto the roof of the palace. She was standing on a large stone turret, about twenty feet in diameter. She was able to peer through gaps in the side all the way around, giving her an unobstructed view of the entire city of Gillodel—and it was breathtaking.

To both east and west there lay rolling hills, as far as her eyes could see. To the north she saw the bustling city, teeming with life. But she didn't look south. She had been trapped in the south of Gillodel, waking and sleeping, for the past five years. She was tired of looking south and unless he was in the Forest of Ćerianell (extremely unlikely), looking south wasn't going to help her find her brother.

She fixed her gaze northward and there she stood, looking out over the city, until the sun was directly overhead. Her stomach told her it was past lunchtime, so she crawled back down into the tower and descended the stairs to the palace below.

Emberlynn stopped a maid she passed in the corridor. The woman appeared to be in her early thirties and the princess thought she looked familiar.

"Do you know if Banning is still here?" Emberlynn asked.

"Yes, Your Highness. He's having lunch with your uncle and cousin as we speak. Shall I go and fetch him?"

"No! I mean...no, no thank you, Tara. It's Tara isn't it?"

"Yes, Your Highness."

"Yes, I remember from visiting before. You've worked here for a long time, then?"

"Oh yes, Your Highness. Since I was just sixteen."

"First of all, call me Emberlynn. Please."

"Are you sure, Miss?"

"Positive."

"As you wish...Emberlynn."

She grinned as she said this.

"And secondly, would you please tell Banning that I'm not at all well and I won't be seeing anyone today."

"You look quite well to me, Miss Emberlynn."

"Yes, but would you please tell Banning that I am not?"

Tara laughed.

"Guy trouble? I understand; I'll let him know."

"Thanks, Tara."

"You're welcome. Emberlynn."

The princess grinned and went back to her room. There was a tray of food waiting for her, which she devoured hungrily. About an hour later there was a knock at the door.

"Come in," she called.

"Beg your pardon, Miss," said Tara, opening the door slowly. "I thought you might like to know that your fiancé left a few minutes ago. He shouldn't be back again until the morning."

"Thank you. I would very much like to know that," grinned Emberlynn.

Tara bowed and left the room, Emberlynn at her heels. She grabbed her cloak on her way out the door and fastened it around her shoulders.

"I'm going to have a walk 'round the city," she said, closing the door behind her. "Would you mind covering for me?"

"Of course not. And it should be easy enough for you to slip out, what with all the people running around on wedding business."

"That's exactly what I'm counting on."

"This is kind of exciting," Tara confessed. "Helping you sneak around like this."

"Then I'll do one better. How would you like to come with me?"

"Are you sure? I mean, don't you need me to stay and cover for you?"

"You know they probably won't check on me until just before supper. If we're back in an hour or so they won't even notice."

"Alright, then. It's like a proper adventure!"

The pair nicked another cloak on the way out, this one a deep purple. Tara put it on and the girls slipped out the front door unnoticed.

When they reached the shops, Emberlynn began looking around. She was taking in her surroundings and making mental notes of any place that looked like you might be able to hide someone. She wasn't having much luck.

"Are you looking for something in particular?" Tara asked.

"Yes and no."

"Maybe I can help. I grew up in Faryn—my family runs the bookshop there, but I've lived here in Gillodel for fifteen years."

Emberlynn gave her a quizzical look but did not mention her time in Faryn. Instead she asked the most pressing question on her mind.

"Tara, what do you know about Duke Theron?"

"Oh goodness, Miss."

The princess shot her a stern look.

"Emberlynn, I mean."

Emberlynn smiled.

"I guess I know a bit about him, but..."

"But what?"

"But I really shouldn't say. We're not supposed to talk about it."

"Just tell me one thing. What did he do before he became duke?"

"Doing some research on the future father-in-law, are you?"

"Something like that..."

"He was the royal scribe."

"Interesting."

They walked around the city for a bit longer, before returning to the palace. Emberlynn didn't find any leads, but she wasn't giving up hope. She would just have to keep looking.

The princess decided to join her family for dinner that evening.

"Lovely to see you, Emberlynn!" Thomas exclaimed as she entered the dining hall.

"I hope this means you're feeling better," said Damian.

She took a seat beside him and said, "I am, thank you. I think I just needed to rest."

"You've been through a lot," he replied, kissing the top of her head. "But you're safe now."

But she knew that nothing could be further from the truth. There was no way Theron and Banning had failed to figure out that she had remembered everything. They were probably wondering why she hadn't turned them in yet, but surely they would know that she had no proof. After her behavior toward Jack—err...Aaver...the night before, it would be easy to discredit her by saying she had been tricked, or even brainwashed. They were probably at Whitehawk that very moment concocting some sort of scheme. Whatever it was, she had to find Aedyn before they had a chance to carry it out.

The conversation over dinner was a bit awkward, as no one wanted to bring up the subject of her "kidnapping" or say anything that might stir up unpleasant memories. The Lemethian royal family mostly just talked amongst themselves, occasionally asking Emberlynn how she cared for the soup or the chicken. Finally Emberlynn had enough and asked Damian about his wedding.

"I can't believe you're getting married in two days! Is everything ready to go?"

Her cousin tried the best to hide the sadness in his eyes, but Emberlynn saw it buried underneath his best poker face; she knew a thing or two about hiding one's sadness. With everything that had been going on she had almost forgotten about what had transpired between Damian and Kinleigh the night of the ball. He had tried to find her in the days that followed but there was no record of a Kinleigh anywhere in Lemeth. He told himself it was for the best; it wouldn't have changed the fact that he was going to marry Sierra of Tardyn. He had no choice, but, of course, Emberlynn knew none of this.

"I believe so. Sierra will be arriving tomorrow with her father. Other than that, my mother has taken care of everything."

"I just want everything to be perfect for my only son's wedding," Alette said.

"And so it will be," Thomas replied.

"I'm so glad you're here for it," Damian said, turning to Emberlynn. "I'm not sure I could have done it without you," he added in a whisper.

"Trust me, I know," she responded. "I have a fiancé of my own, remember?"

"And I don't love mine either," she thought.

∽

After dinner the princess headed up to her room, but not without making a few stops along the way. She crept silently to the east wing of the castle, stopping when she saw a large iron door. The guards changed shifts just after supper so she knew this would be her best chance. Sure enough, two men were standing in front of the door in friendly conversation.

"Is the supper good tonight?" one asked.

"Yeah, there's some mutton left over from upstairs."

"Very nice. Been a while since I had mutton."

"They're pulling out all the stops ever since the princess turned up."

"It'll only get better, what with the prince's wedding this week."

Emberlynn heard all this from behind the pillar where she was hiding. She didn't fancy the idea of waiting around all day for them to finish their rousing mutton conversation, so she took off one of her shoes and threw it at a suit of armor a few feet down the corridor.

"What was that?!" asked the first man.

"I don't know. But I'm not on duty, am I?" replied the second.

"Oh, come on!"

The two men scurried down the hall toward the sound. Seizing this chance, Emberlynn sprang out from behind the pillar, opened the iron door, slipped through, and closed it quickly behind her.

The princess had never been in this part of the castle, but she knew what lay at the bottom of the staircase she now found herself in front of. She took a deep breath and hurried quietly down. When she reached the bottom it took her eyes a moment to adjust to the light. It was dark and damp, and the air was stale. She could hear the quiet drip as drops of water leaked from one corner of the ceiling, falling into a puddle below.

She walked close to the wall as she crept down the dingy hallway. There were empty cells on either side of her, their iron bars dark as the feeling this place gave her. Emberlynn came 'round a curve and saw him, standing in a cell at the very end of the room staring into the shadows.

"Aaver!" she cried quietly, running toward him.

"What are you doing here?!" asked a threatening voice.

She now saw the guard standing in the shadows by the door. He stepped out of the darkness and put himself between his prisoner and the princess.

"I am Emberlynn, Princess of Ardia. I may go wherever I please," she said defiantly, head held high.

"Sorry, Highness," he said. "I didn't recognize you at first."

"Well now that you do, kindly step out of my way."

"I'm afraid I can't do that."

"And why not?"

"I'm under strict orders from King Thomas that no one is to be allowed near the prisoner, least of all you."

She stared at him intently before deciding that he wasn't going to back down. Then she turned her eyes past him to the man in the cell beyond. He met her gaze and held up his hands, miming the motion of an opening a book. She nodded, a faint look of confusion tracing the lines of her face. Then she turned her gaze back to the guard.

"Very well," she said, finally. "But you're under strict orders from me not to tell anyone I came here."

"Yes, Your Highness," he said, bowing.

She hurried back down the hallway, up the stairs, and through the great iron door.

"Not a word to anyone!" she ordered, as she walked past the main guard.

He nodded.

The library was exactly how it had been the night of the ball, with one exception—the *Chronicles of the Kingdom* had been placed back amongst the myriad of other books that lined the walls of the beautiful room.

She was hesitant to light any of the big candles spread around the library, as she didn't want to draw any attention to herself. If Theron had been the palace scribe, he would have had full access to the palace library. In fact, he would have spent the majority of his time there. At this point she felt like she was grasping at straws, but maybe there was something here that would give her a clue as to Aedyn's whereabouts. Besides, this was the last place he was before being taken to the garden.

The princess walked around with her small candle, reading the titles of the books within its glow. She did this for about ten minutes, finding nothing of interest. Then she heard the sound of footsteps, followed by the smallest creak. She had heard that sound before. Luckily, she was standing in the back corner of the library near a giant ladder. She wedged herself quickly between the ladder and the bookshelf, blowing out her candle as she did so. It didn't provide much cover, but it was better than nothing.

As soon as the flame from her candle was out, another one appeared in the room. It emerged from the garden passageway and revealed two dark figures. She knew who it was before they spoke.

"Alright, hurry up," whispered Theron. "And remember, if anyone sees you just tell them you were hoping to sneak a few moments with your fiancé, whom you haven't spent any time with since her return."

"Yes Father, I know," Banning replied, rolling his eyes in the darkness. I'll be back in a moment."

Banning tiptoed across the library and out into the corridor beyond. Theron waited. Emberlynn managed to steady her breathing and stay perfectly still, but she was worried he would hear her heart pounding in her chest. He didn't. He was too busy pacing silently around the room, anxious for Banning to return. When he finally did, he let out a great sigh.

"She's not there."

"What do you mean she's not there?"

"She's not in her room. I put a sleep charm on the guard and went in. She wasn't there."

"Clever, clever girl."

"Now what? It's only a matter of time before she rats us out."

"If Emberlynn was going to turn us in I believe she would have done so by now. Obviously, she has her reasons for keeping it to herself."

"Like not wanting people to think she's lost her mind?"

"Well that's a pretty good reason, but I believe there's more. She has something up her sleeve, some plan we aren't seeing."

"You don't sound too worried about that fact."

"Oh, let her make her silly plans. It will make this whole thing so much more interesting, and that much more satisfying when we claim the victory."

Emberlynn felt her blood begin to boil but remained perfectly still in a silent rage. Theron wanted someone who would fight back? Good; that's exactly what he was going to get.

"Should we wait a few hours for Emberlynn to return to her room?"

"I'm afraid we're not going to have any luck tonight. She's not so easy a prey as poor brother dearest."

The princess' face was crimson and she gripped the ladder, willing herself to stay put.

"No, Son. We're going to have to tackle this one head on."

"And how exactly are we going to do that?"

"Don't worry. I have an idea —for another day. Come along, now..."

The pair slunk back through the passageway, leaving Emberlynn alone in the dark.

She sat there for a moment, catching her breath. When she finally composed herself, she slipped out from behind the ladder. The princess couldn't see much in the darkness, but as she shuffled across the library, she noticed a book lying on the table. She was unable to make out the title but she had a feeling it was important. Stashing it under her dress, she crept quietly out of the library and headed back to her room.

⁓

The sun had long been awake when Emberlynn heard a knock on her bedroom door. She was sitting at the foot of her bed curled up with a book. Well, it wasn't a book exactly, rather

207

a book of books. The princess had stumbled across a catalog of all the books in the palace library. Admittedly she was a tad disappointed upon returning to her room the night before to discover this was her "important book" from the library table. But she didn't want to sleep; she wasn't ready to face her brother yet. At least it gave her something to do.

"Come in."

"Morning, Emberlynn!" Tara said cheerily, as she opened the door.

"Good morning, Tara," she replied, looking up from her book.

"Your uncle was wondering if you would be joining them for breakfast. Well, actually your fiancé was wondering, but I'm to say it's the king."

"I'm afraid I'm still asleep."

"Ahhh, yes I can see that. Is there anything you might want when you're not asleep?"

"I imagine I'd fancy a cup of tea. Maybe some ham on a biscuit."

"I'll bring that right up and, uhhh, leave it by the bedside for when you wake," Tara giggled.

"Thanks, Tara!" said Emberlynn, smiling.

"I'm so not in the mood for that!" she exclaimed, once Tara was gone. "Nor this," she added, putting the book down.

She started to close it when something caught her eye.

Magic and Myth.

"*That's odd,*" she thought. "*I can't imagine there are all that many books about magic. How strange that it would turn up here as well.*"

She marked down the location of the book. Then she washed up and dressed. Tara returned momentarily with a plate of food, which she gobbled down before heading to the library. Emberlynn placed the catalog back on the table then headed to the indicated location. It wasn't there. The princess spent the better part of an hour scouring the shelves only to find the same thing.

"*Why would it be marked in the catalog but not be in the library?*" she wondered.

Perhaps there was only one copy of the book—the one she had seen before.

"*If that's the case, how did it end up in a small bookshop in Faryn?*"

Emberlynn thought this seemed rather strange.

When she left the library she had intended to head back to her room, but on the way there she changed her mind. She had spent far too much time hiding away. She was never going to accomplish anything if she didn't get out and do a bit of legwork. So instead of heading off to the guest wing, she went downstairs and walked casually into the sitting room where her aunt was going over some last-minute wedding details.

"Morning, Aunt Alette!"

"Good morning, dear. You're just in time! Princess Sierra should be arriving any time now with her father. I can't wait for you to meet her."

"I look forward to it. I've heard she's quite beautiful."

"She certainly is. Of course she doesn't hold a candle to our Emberlynn."

The princess blushed.

"While we're waiting, why don't we have a fitting for your dress?"

"What dress?" Emberlynn asked.

"For Damian's wedding, of course. We can't have the princess of Ardia in a secondhand dress for a royal wedding. Elaine!"

An older woman came running into the sitting room. Emberlynn assumed this was Elaine.

"Yes, Your Highness?"

"Elaine, can you bring Emberlynn's dress please? We need to see how it fits."

"Right away, ma'am!"

She scurried out of the room and returned momentarily with a green satin dress trimmed in gold. They slipped it over Emberlynn's head and she suppressed a gag, for two reasons. First the dress was far too glitzy. She was a princess, so she liked a little glitz and a little poof, but this dress crossed the line. It was death by glitz. Poof-ageddon. The second reason was because as soon they'd slipped the dress on, Banning walked in the room.

"No boys!" Elaine cried. "Off with you!"

Emberlynn shot him a taunting smirk as Elaine shut the door in his face.

"What do you think?" asked her aunt.

"Well the coloring is to die for!" she replied honestly, surveying her reflection in the large mirror Elaine had brought in. "But would you mind if I make a few tweaks?"

The dress had clearly been designed by someone who didn't know her.

"Not at all," said Elaine, looking slightly dejected. "Just tell me what you'd like me to change and I'll do it."

"I was actually thinking I could do it," Emberlynn replied.

Alette and Elaine stared at her, dumbfounded.

"I didn't know you could sew," her aunt said, finally.

"Neither did I, until recently. But I'm actually pretty good at it, and I quite enjoy it."

"Well then, just let me pin where it needs to be taken in, and you can have at it," said Elaine.

"Are you sure you don't mind?" Emberlynn asked.

"Not a bit. This means I have the afternoon off," she said, grinning.

"And a well-deserved one, at that," said Alette. "You've done a lovely job on the dresses, Elaine."

"Thank you, Your Highness."

Elaine put a few pins in the dress, then curtseyed and hurried out of the room to begin her day off. Emberlynn shimmied out of her gown, dressed again, then set about work on the alterations. She planned to take away most of the poof and raise the waistline considerably. She was just getting started when Tara rushed in.

"Your Highness! Princess Sierra has just arrived!"

"Thank you, Tara," replied Alette, standing up and smoothing her dress. "Emberlynn, let's go and greet our guests."

CHAPTER 22

THE KEY

Princess Sierra of Tardyn was nothing like Emberlynn had expected. She was a tall woman—thin, but with notable curves. Her long red curls fell just above her waist, the color a stark contrast to her porcelain skin and bright blue eyes. Her lips, which she wore in a slight pout, were stained red.

"But she's not being snobby," Emberlynn noted. *"She's sad."*

The Lemethian royal family was lined up, along with Emberlynn, Theron, and Banning, to greet her in the front hall of the palace. Damian walked to her and kissed her hand.

"Welcome back," he said, sweetly but without much conviction.

Sierra smiled sadly.

"Thank you, Damian," she said softly. "This is my brother, Kieron," she added, motioning to the man beside her.

He closely resembled his sister, but Emberlynn guessed he was a few years older.

Damian clasped Kieron's hand as King Thomas welcomed their entire party to Lemeth.

"Was your father unable to join you?" Thomas inquired. "I was hoping he would have been well enough to make the journey."

Sierra's bottom lip began to quiver, but she took a deep breath and kept her composure. Only now did Emberlynn notice that her eyes were red from days of crying.

"I'm so sorry," she said, stepping forward and taking Sierra's hand. "I'm Emberlynn of Ardia. Damian is my cousin," she added.

Sierra nodded.

"Yes, I know. We heard of your return and are happy for it."

"What's going on?" asked the king.

"Our father passed away last week," Kieron replied, sadly.

"Good heavens! I had no idea."

"He was sick for some time, but we did not know the extent of it. He bore it well, nobly, but..." Kieron trailed off.

"He was a great man and an old friend," said Thomas. "He will be missed."

Everyone knew this was not entirely true; relations between Lemeth and Tardyn had been fairly volatile for generations. This marriage was an attempt at remedying that, and their best hope for lasting peace. But King Thomas and King Kierr of Tardyn had been on diplomatic terms for the past few years, and his children appreciated the sentiment.

"Are you sure you want to go through with the wedding?" Emberlynn asked Sierra.

This was met with many disapproving looks.

"Wouldn't it maybe be better to postpone it for a bit, until you've had some time to mourn?"

"I did consider that," Sierra replied. "But you've already gone through all this trouble, and I've had my dress made. We've come all this way. And...well, it just seemed silly to put off the inevitable," she said, almost inaudibly. "Besides, it's what father wanted. And Kieron feels the best way to honor him is to fulfill his last wish."

"Of course," said Thomas. "Rightly so."

He looked relieved.

"Don't worry, King Thomas," Kieron assured him, "Nothing will stand in the way of this marriage, or the alliance of our kingdoms."

Thomas clasped him by the hand and said, "Long live King Kieron of Tardyn."

"Long live King Kieron!" echoed the others.

"Well enough standing around," said queen Alette. "Would you care for something to eat?" she asked her guests. "It's nearly lunchtime."

With that, the party moved into the great hall where a small feast was waiting for them. Emberlynn sat by Sierra and asked her all about Tardyn, leaving Damian to entertain Banning. Her cousin did not seem to mind.

After lunch Emberlynn showed the Tardynians to the guest wing and left them to rest from their journey. Then she headed back down to finish the alterations on her gown. This only took a few hours, and she was finished before dinner.

The rest of the evening was something of a blur. Kieron joined them for dinner, but Sierra dined in her room; apparently it was bad luck for Damian to see his bride the evening before their wedding. Emberlynn ate quickly then retired to her chambers.

"*What was Aaver trying to tell me?*" she pondered.

She'd spent the greater part of the last day wondering just that. Surely, he'd intended for her to go to the library. He, of all people, would have known about Theron's past. What had he meant for her to find there?

"Or is this about Magic and Myth? We did look over it at the shop together. Maybe there's something I missed?"

But surely that was too great a coincidence. Aaver had no way of knowing that book had ever been in the palace library. So maybe this is was about the night of the ball—something Theron or Banning had said in the library.

"Oh, I don't know. I don't know at all."

Emberlynn paced back and forth in her room until long after the sun had gone to bed. Eventually she did the same. She dreamed that night of everything that had passed in the last five years: moments, conversations, horrible revelations...all like pieces to a puzzle jumbled up inside her head. She couldn't make sense of any of it.

♎

Back in Faryn, the concern of Aaver's parents had been growing. Their son had disappeared two days before, leaving nothing but a note.

> Gone with Hannah.
> Trust me.
> -A

They didn't know what this meant, but it clearly wasn't a good sign.

"What trouble could sweet Hannah have gotten herself into?" asked his mother.

"I don't know, Ćeidei," he replied, for this was her real name.

His was Aaron; their daughter's Audrianna.

"Maybe we should go after them," she said.

215

"We don't even know where they've gone."

"Actually, I think we do," Audrianna interjected, as she walked quickly into the kitchen.

She was holding a small metal object in her hand: Emberlynn's royal crest.

"Where did you get that?!" Aaron asked.

"Hannah's bedside drawer. I was looking for the book Mother lent her on sewing. This was hidden beneath it."

"I knew she seemed familiar," said Ćeidei. "How did I not know?"

"She's grown up since then, sweetheart. You can't blame yourself for that."

"But if she's gone off to take attend to a family matter, then..."

"Then we need to leave. Now," Aaron stated.

✺

The next morning Emberlynn opened her eyes with the sun. She washed and dressed before heading downstairs for an early breakfast. After all, a long night of troubled dreams is a sure-fire way for a girl to work up an appetite. On a normal day if she'd risen at this hour, she would have been the only person walking around the palace; however, this was not a normal day.

The palace was bustling with people running about, tending to last minute wedding details. She saw food being carried, armfuls of fabric and flowers, and even a rather large chicken being chased down the corridor. There was nothing like a Lemethian wedding.

She reached the dining hall, expecting to be the only one there. She was mistaken.

When she opened the door, she heard a loud cry and was in the arms of her mother before she realized what was happening. Her father was close behind, wrapping his wife and daughter in a monstrous hug.

"Where have you been, my darling girl?" King Edric asked, wiping a tear from his eye.

"There's plenty of time for stories later, Father," Emberlynn promised. "For the time being, take my word that I am well and unharmed, and let's place the focus where it should be—on Damian and Sierra."

"Quite right, dear one," was his reply.

The king kissed his daughter on the top of her head and pulled her close once more, saying more in his silence than words ever could.

Once things had settled down a bit, they ate breakfast then rushed off to get ready for the wedding. Emberlynn headed upstairs to her chambers and has almost reached them when she heard crying coming from the room next door. She knocked on the door and let herself in.

"Are you alright?" she asked the sobbing redhead.

"Oh, Emberlynn! Hi," sniffed Sierra, quickly drying her eyes. "Yes, I'm...I'm fine."

"You miss your father, don't you?"

"Very much. But that's not why I'm crying."

"Do you want to talk about it?" she asked, sitting down on the bed beside her.

"You know how these things are," Sierra answered, vaguely.

"Royal weddings, you mean?"

"Royal marriages. Well, then again, maybe you don't."

"Banning isn't quite as he seems on the surface," Emberlynn replied, catching her meaning.

"Really? How so?"

"I think that's a conversation best saved for another day."

"Fair enough."

"For what it's worth, though, Damian is pretty great. I know I'm a bit partial, but..."

"I'm sorry, I didn't mean to imply—"

"I know you didn't. I just wanted to give him a good reference."

This made Sierra laugh.

"I understand why my father wanted this and why my brother is carrying out his wishes. It's what's best for Tardyn and a princess' duty is always to do what's best for her kingdom."

Emberlynn nodded in agreement.

"It's just...well sometimes duty means sacrifice."

"What's his name?" asked Emberlynn, beginning to understand.

"Names aren't important," replied Sierra, smiling sadly. "What's past is past. And this..." she said, gazing out the window, "is my future."

"I'm sorry."

"Thank you. I suppose you and I will be family soon. I'll be glad to have you as my friend."

"Of course," said Emberlynn, standing to leave. "Let me know if you need anything."

She went next door to her own chambers where two hand-maidens were waiting to help her prepare for the wedding. The others crowded in the room next door, fussing over the bride-to-be.

❧

Charlie was sitting in the dungeon outside the single oc-cupied cell, his back to the wall. It was his turn to guard the prisoner and he wasn't too pleased about it. The other guards, who were manning the throne room, were able to attend the royal wedding. He, however, was stuck in a dingy pit with a convicted criminal—not exactly his idea of a perfect day.

He sat there, listening to the *drip, drip, drip* from the ceiling, when all of a sudden, he heard another sound: footsteps. "Who goes there?!" he demanded, un-sheathing his sword and trying to sound menacing. He stepped out of the shadows and, next thing he knew, found himself waking up on the damp stone floor. The cell was empty.

൭

Just before sunset all three royal families, along with all the Lemethian nobles and servants who worked in the palace, gathered in the throne room. The sight was breathtaking: tiny white blossoms were placed painstakingly around the room, along with clumps of Snowberries. There was a long red velvet carpet lining the aisle where the bride would be walking. Everyone was dressed in their absolute best—all wearing brightly colored gowns or shirts (even the servants had been made special frocks for the occasion), and the royals were adorned with glittering jewels.

Emberlynn was standing beside her parents near the front of the hall when it happened. Banning strutted over to her and said the last thing she was excepting to hear.

"Emberlynn, darling..."

"Yes?" she asked, forcing a smile.

"We have waited such a long time for our day. I've missed you so dearly in your absence, and I can't bear the thought of waiting any longer. Our families are already gathered..."

Her eyes widened in horror. She knew what was coming.

"Would you marry me here, today? After Damian's wedding is through, of course."

"What a marvelous idea!" King Edric exclaimed. "Let me go speak with the priest."

Banning reached up to touch Emberlynn's face in what seemed to be a romantic gesture. But the princess smacked his hand away before doing something no one expected.

"No," she cried. "Absolutely not!"

"Come on, Emberlynn," sighed Edric. "Not again!"

She ran out of the hall before anyone could stop her and had disappeared before anyone saw where she went. Her father was dumbfounded, but Banning was feeling quite pleased with himself. So maybe his attempt at a little mind control had backfired. Still...without a proper reason, she'd never be able to evade the marriage forever. Sooner or later it would happen, probably that very day. Her father would insist, and someday Banning, son of Theron, would be king of Ardia.

♋

Emberlynn didn't know where she was going, she simply ran. Her feet took her to the only natural place—the place where it all began. She walked across the garden, thinking about all the things that had happened since that fateful night five years before. But somehow fate always brought her back to this place. As she walked the length of the garden the sun began its descent, setting the sky on fire as Snow White's stars shone down from the heavens. She saw a light coming from the Western edge of the garden, as something caught the sky fire. And suddenly her whole world was set ablaze.

Emberlynn felt the world freeze around her as the final puzzle piece fell into place.

Click.

She smacked her palm against her forehead.

"Idiot!" she cried. "Idiot!"

She ran to the silver fountain as fast as her legs would carry her. How could she not have noticed before? The way the fountain caught the light—it was cast with fairy dust. And Emberlynn was, she had finally figured out, allergic to fairy dust. Which is why she sneezed uncontrollably whenever she was around it; why she had sneezed the night of the ball when she had dipped her hand in. It wasn't because of the cold at all.

The answer had been there all along, right under her nose.

"The magical properties of water..." she said, suddenly, to no one in particular. "I did miss something in the book. Well done, Aaver!"

With that she pulled the key from beneath her dress, took a deep breath, and dived headfirst into the fountain.

Emberlynn kept swimming down, key in hand, wondering where the bottom was. When she finally reached it, she looked around. The water was dark, yet perfectly clear. She saw a small light coming from the base of the fountain. She swam to it and found the source of the light—a small keyhole. Without hesitation, she took the key and placed it into the lock. If she wasn't already doing so, she would have been holding her breath.

She turned the key and heard a faint click. Suddenly Emberlynn found herself engulfed in light. She knew what was coming next before it happened, but she couldn't do anything stop it. The princess sneezed with great force, and water filled her mouth. She couldn't see anything, couldn't breathe, and found herself sinking. This was it, Emberlynn knew—she was drowning. She had probably just saved her kingdom and secured her true love's pardon, but she wouldn't live to see any of it.

As the last tiny bubble of air left the princess' lungs, she felt an arm wrap suddenly around her waist, pulling her upward. Emberlynn managed a weak smile; she knew these arms. As her head finally cleared the surface, she tried to take a breath, but couldn't. She grabbed onto the side of the fountain and coughed until she had expelled all the water from her lungs. Then she took in a deep, life-giving breath, and opened her eyes.

Beside her in the water was her brother. She laughed and climbed out of the fountain. Aedyn did the same, standing beside his sister and taking everything in as if he was seeing the world for the first time. Emberlynn threw her arms forcefully around him, shedding tears of joy onto his already sopping wet shoulder. After a minute she pulled away.

"And now, for act two..."

The sun was setting, the sky filled with fire, and the wedding just beginning. Damian stood at the front of the hall looking at his bride, who was preparing to walk down the aisle. The court musicians struck up the waltz. The prince saw King Edric and Queen Gwyneria, and he wondered why his cousin wasn't with them. He scanned the crowd and, after a moment, saw her enter the room, dripping wet, accompanied by...no...it couldn't be. It wasn't possible, but...

The crowd began to murmur as they noticed the strange scene. The music faltered as the musicians, too, stopped to stare. The chaos suddenly gave way to complete and utter silence, as people realized who they were looking at.

"Congratulations, cousin!" said Aedyn, grinning, as the pair finally reached the front of the room, leaving a trail of water behind them. "You didn't think I'd miss your wedding, did you?"

The entire royal family stood blank-faced and slack-jawed. After a few moment's silence, Damian made his way slowly toward them. He stared intently at Aedyn's face then grinned suddenly, throwing his arms around him.

"Aedyn!" he cried. "But what? How? And...why...why are you two wet?"

His parents, too, rushed forward for a reunion that would have been even more touching than Emberlynn's, had they not been interrupted by Banning and his father as they came bursting through the crowd.

"Aedyn!" called the Duke, trying his best to feign happiness. "So relieved to have you back, dear boy. We feared the worst after your disappearance. Such a tragedy..."

He undoubtedly would have said more, but Aedyn stopped him with a swift punch to the ribcage. Theron doubled over and fell to the floor. When he had caught his breath, he looked up at Aedyn.

"Highness, your absence must have driven you mad. Should you not be attacking your captor? There he is now!"

Indeed, at that very moment Aaver entered the throne room, his father at his side. Ceidei and Audrianna followed closely behind.

Theron had hoped to make his escape while Aedyn was distracted, but he wasn't quick enough.

"Arrogant old man!" retorted the prince, pinning him down and spitting on his face. "Do you think me a fool? I remember plainly all the details of my capture and imprisonment at your hand!"

There was an audible gasp from all present. Aedyn attempted to kick Theron in the chest, but this time the older man was ready for him. The Duke grabbed his leg and threw him to the ground with ease.

Damian stepped in to defend his cousin, drawing his sword at pointing it at Theron.

"Silly boy," said the Duke, patronizingly. "I would not do that if I were you."

Damian took a step toward him but he merely put out his hand, palm facing forward, and the prince's sword flew from his hand.

"How did you do that?" Damian asked, glaring at him cautiously.

"I am not as weak as I may appear."

At this he held out his hand again and Damian himself went flying. He crashed into the wall, losing consciousness.

"Enough!" bellowed King Thomas, standing up. "Guards, seize them!" he ordered, pointing at Theron and Banning.

The two exchanged a knowing look and turned to face their assailants. As the guards rushed toward them, they both held up their hands in the same palm-out motion. Five guards fell to the ground, dropping their swords with a loud *crash*!

The wedding guests were screaming as they huddled together in corners and pressed themselves against the walls. Ćeidei and Audrianna stood back with them, but Aaver and Aaron rushed forward.

"Look who finally decided to fight back," Theron sneered.

He pointed his hand toward Aaron and a rushing wind began swirling around the room. It picked up flowers, Snowberries, and spears as it headed toward him. Aaron stepped toward the whirlwind, snapping his fingers. The air was suddenly calm and all the debris fell to the ground.

"Impossible," said Theron, in disbelief.

"Come now, Theron. You're an educated man," said Aaron.

"Oh, of course. All Lemethian nobles came from some-where. You're a descendant of Snow White."

"And you are not."

"No. I'm afraid the blood in these veins flows from a much more... sinister source."

"When did you realize?"

"That the heroes of history weren't the only ones to pass along their talents? Or that I was of one such bloodline? Either way, I think you can guess the general time frame. Being the palace scribe has such benefits. You have access to so much information, and you learn all sorts of things you never knew before. For example..."

Theron shoved both hands through the air toward Aaron, forming a semi-transparent forcefield around him. Aaron beat on the sides of it but was unable to escape, or even make a sound.

"Did you really mean to stand around talking all night? BO-RING!"

Aaver stepped toward the duke, who laughed and nodded to his son. Banning lifted his hand toward Aaver in the familiar palm-out motion, but nothing happened. He stopped for a sec-ond, a confused look on his face, before trying again; he didn't realize Aaver was blocking his magic. Aaver rolled his eyes and walked straight up to him, punching him square in the face and knocking him unconscious. Two Lemethian guards ran over and grabbed Banning, ready to restrain him when he awoke.

"Oh, very nice," said Theron with a sinister grin. "Come and play with the big dogs."

Aaver lifted his hand, shooting sparks at the duke. Theron merely stepped to the side. In response, the duke sent a force-field at him like the one that held his father. Aaver reached up and grabbed the forcefield with his hands, ripping it apart and stepping through.

"I'm impressed. You could teach daddy a few things."

From behind his cage, Aaron snarled something at Theron that nobody could hear.

Theron sneered at Aver and raised his hand toward a large chandelier at the center of the room. It creaked ominously for a moment. A slow web of cracks began to appear in the ceiling, forming a circle around the chandelier. Suddenly it ripped free, plummeting at a startling speed toward Aaver. He managed to redirect it, setting it down beside him, away from the cowering wedding guests. Then he turned to Theron.

A fire burned in Aaver's eyes and, moments later, that same fire manifested itself in the palms of his hands. It cracked and flickered as he eyed his assailant. He took a deep breath before sweeping both hands straight out in front of him, aiming a blast at Theron's chest.

Theron dove out of the way, falling to the floor in an undignified heap. He sat up, hatred radiating from him, and sparks crackling at the tips of his fingers. He snapped them, and a blast of lightning cascaded down upon Aaver. The moment before it made contact, Aaver was able to summon a shield; the full force of the blast was deflected, scorching a hole in the wall at the far end of the hall and causing several tapestries to fall in tatters to the ground. After a moment, Aaver released the shield and stood to his feet, winded but unmarked.

Without missing a beat, Theron pulled the air in front of him at invisible strings, causing Aaver's feet to slip out from under him. Aaver fell back to the ground with a loud *crash*, rolling to the side just as Theron sent a second blast to the place he had been just moments before.

Aaver jumped to his feet and turned to Theron.

"You're quick, boy—I'll give you that. But you're out of your depth here," Theron said. "Stand down and your life shall end quickly and with little pain. I may even allow you to keep it. It would be a shame for you to be reunited with your lost love after all this time, only to be taken away from her."

At the mention of Emberlynn, Aaver's vision went red. Not only had Theron been the cause of their separation, but he had the gall to stand there and taunt him about it.

"You did not defeat me as a child, and you shall not defeat me now," Aaver replied, his blood boiling.

Theron shot third blast of lighting at Aaver, which he swatted out of the way, grinning. Something in Aaver had snapped; he was done playing games.

"What do you hope to accomplish here, Theron? Your plans have been uncovered and undone. You have lost all power here at court; you and your puppet of a son will never have the throne, of Ardia or Lemeth."

The scowl on Theron's face faltered almost impreceptibly as he considered Aaver's point, but he quickly regained his composure.

"It is true," he admitted, "that what I seek can no longer be achieved through subtlety or deceit. But no matter. There is always a path to power for those with the strength to reach out and take it."

With these words, Theron turned to King Thomas and raised his hand toward him. For a moment nothing happened. Then the king began sliding swiftly across the floor of the hall straight toward Theron. Aaver stepped in front of the king, breaking the pull that Theron had on him. Thomas fell backward, the breath knocked from his lungs. Aaver stood, arms crossed, between Theron and his prey, rooted to the spot. After a few silent moments, he stepped forward, distracting Theron as Thomas raised himself up and retreated back against the wall, placing himself firmly in front of his wife.

"You never learn," Aaver said, matter-of-factly. "If you want to get to the royal family, you'll have to go through me."

"I intend to, boy," Theron spat.

He surveyed Aaver, his eyes traveling up and down, searching for any sign of weakness. Without warning, he lunged forward.

Somehow Emberlynn knew what he was going to do before it happened. She had just enough time to pick up a sword and run to meet him. As Theron dove at Aaver, he summoned a sword to himself, which he pointed at his opponent's throat. The princess dived between them, twisting Theron's sword around and knocking it from his hands. The onlookers gasped. Theron smacked her square across the face. As Emberlynn collapsed on the ground, he turned back to Aaver.

The moment Emberlynn hit the floor, something triggered in her memory. The world faded away and she found herself lying on the forest floor in a pale pink dress. She tried to focus through the haze and, finally, made out the figures of Theron and Aaver standing beside her.

"As for you..." Theron said, smacking Aaver across the face and knocking him to the ground beside Emberlynn, "No one will believe the son of a kidnapper."

Everything faded to darkness, and when she came to and opened her eyes, she saw Aaver kneeling over her. She heard the sound of footsteps and knew someone was coming. Aaver didn't have much time. He was holding a something small and metal, and the princess saw a golden light flow from his hand into the object. It glowed for a moment then faded. Aaver unclasped the chain around Emberlynn's neck and pulled the charm off it, stashing it in his pocket. It was a small silver star.

Then he strung this new object on the chain, fastened it around her neck, and tucked it back inside her dress. It was the key.

The footsteps grew louder, and he knew it was time to go.

"Goodbye, Emmie. I'll never forget you..." he whispered, kissing her softly on the forehead.

Then he turned and ran. Before her eyes closed one last time, she saw Theron standing over her, flanked by a group of Lemethian guards.

Her eyes shot open and she sat up. Her brother, Aedyn, was kneeling protectively beside her. She squeezed his hand and smiled. She had finally realized what had happened, and she knew precisely how to end it.

Theron and Aaver were firing spells at each other, to no avail; they were too equally matched.

"Aaver!" Emberlynn shouted!

He turned to her as she broke the chain off her neck, taking the key and tossing it to him. It was as if the world was moving in slow motion. As he caught it a golden light flowed from it, lighting up his entire body. When the glow faded, he dropped the key to the ground with a *thud*.

Even Theron knew what had just happened. Part of Aaver's magic had resided in the key for the past five years, protecting the girl he loved. He was holding her hand when Theron tried to erase her memory. His magic had kept it from being fully erased. And the key had kept Banning from using his magic on her during their courtship. This is why she only felt the full weight of it when she took the key off on the night of her birthday. Now that Aaver had all his magic, Theron was no longer a match for him. You could see the fear dawn in the duke's eyes.

Theron reached out a hand, and the air in front of him began to ripple. He stepped forward through thin air, disappearing as he did so. But Aaver, who was quick on his feet, reached out, and his arm disappeared into the void. Then he pulled Theron back into the throne room. Aaver's hand was around his throat and he was perfectly still; Aaver had frozen him so he could not move.

The forcefield around Aaron dissolved and he ran to his son, clasping him on the shoulder. The rest of the guards joined them, grabbing the now petrified duke.

"Should we throw these two in the dungeon?" one of them asked.

King Thomas stepped forward.

"This one can create a portal out of thin air," he said, indicating Theron. "I think he can escape a prison cell."

"Clearly this one did," said Damian, who had regained consciousness by this point.

He walked over to Aaver and put his hand on his other shoulder.

"How did you manage it?" he asked.

"My parents broke me out," Aaver grinned.

He pulled Emberlynn's signet ring out of his pocket and tossed it to her. She caught it, laughing silently at her forgetfulness.

"Hey, I helped!" said Audrianna, stepping into the center of the room.

Damian caught her gaze and, as he did so, turned white as a sheet. There was a long pause as the two stared at each other in silent understanding.

"I guess we have our answer," he said finally, walking toward her.

The onlookers assumed he was referring to the means of her brother's escape. Only Aaver and Emberlynn knew what he really meant. Four months ago the princess had thought that true love and magic only existed in the pages of a history book.

But she knew now that both of those things, while rare, were also very real—she had just seen proof. Her heart ached for Audrianna and Damian; to find true love only to have it taken from you was one of the worst things she could imagine.

Emberlynn and Aaver exchanged sad smiles. She and Aedyn stood, still wet from the fountain, and hugged each other. Edric and Gwyneria ran to them, throwing their arms around their children and crying unashamedly. Their family was whole again. Thomas and Alette joined them, as did Damian; such a moment has not been seen since, in any of the three kingdoms.

When the moment passed, Thomas turned to his old friend.

"Aaron," he said, clasping his hand. "Can you forgive me for believing you could ever have done such a terrible thing?"

"Of course. I know how it looked."

"Why did you think it was Aaron?" Emberlynn asked.

"Aedyn's jacket was found in his home—the one he'd been wearing at the ball."

"Planted there, of course, by this snake," Aaron added, pointing to Theron.

"Then when you disappeared as well..." Thomas shuddered. "Well Theron was the one who found you in the woods and brought you back to us. I should have known when you couldn't remember anything that something wasn't right. Theron said it was shock, and we believed him."

Suddenly they heard a great clamor from outside the hall, as Charlie ran in.

"The prisoner has escaped!!" he shouted, out of breath from running.

He stopped when we he saw the strange scene before him.

"Yes, we know..." said King Thomas, laughing. "It's alright, come join the party."

Charlie walked sheepishly in, looking confused, and joined the rest of the guards.

"Why did no one tell me about Aedyn?" Emberlynn asked, when her uncle turned back to her.

"I suppose I'm the person to answer that," answered Edric. "It was my decision. And I think now that it was a wrong one. But you'd been through such trauma already we didn't want to add to it. So I issued an edict that no one in the kingdom was to speak of him. All traces of him were removed from the kingdom. Your uncle did the same..."

Emberlynn nodded.

"I understand."

"But tell me, how on earth did you find him?!" her father asked.

"All in good time, Father," she replied, walking over to Aaver.

"The magical properties of water?" she said, laughing.

"I knew you'd figure it out," he grinned.

"How did you get your hands on the key that unlocked Aedyn's prison?"

"I found it in the garden that night. I guess Theron dropped it."

"Well you saved my life, as well as my brother's and the entire kingdom of Ardia."

"No, Emberlynn. You saved your kingdom all on your own."

"Not on my own," she said, smiling. "Now," she added, loudly. "There are more pressing matters to attend to. First there's these two to deal with."

She nodded toward Theron and Banning.

"And then we have a wedding to attend," added Aedyn. "Where's the blushing bride?"

Sierra's brother and servants had escorted her to the back corner when the battle began. She now walked slowly and tentatively to the center of the room.

"Let's get this place cleaned up," Emberlynn said, noticing the damage the fight had caused to the wedding décor. "While you take care of the snakes."

She looked at Aaver as she said this.

"Happily," Aaver replied. "I know just the thing..." he added, grinning at Aedyn. "Care to help me?"

"With pleasure!"

Aaver picked up the key from the floor and he and Aedyn strolled outside to the garden, followed by a group of guards dragging Theron and Banning.

*

They returned to the hall a little while later to find that it looked almost as it had before the battle. Everything and everyone was slightly more disheveled but, considering the events that had just taken place, it was pretty remarkable.

Aedyn and Aaver walked to the front of the hall and took their place next to Damian, as his best friends. The court musicians began playing and Princess Sierra stood at the end of the long red carpet, escorted by her brother.

"I love you, little poppy," Kieron whispered to his sister, squeezing her hand.

The pair began the long walk down the aisle.

Audrianna stood at the back of the room, watching Sierra with sadness in her eyes.

"Finishing touch..." she whispered.

She raised her hand up, pointing it at the ceiling. Silver sparks began to rain down, disappearing just before they reached the heads of the guests. She caught Damian's gaze one last time, forcing a smile, though her lip quivered. This was her wedding gift to the man she loved. A single tear ran down her cheek. Damian turned away, knowing if he did not that he, too, would begin to cry. When he looked back, she was gone.

Sierra reached the alter and she and Damian became husband and wife.

∽

The celebration that followed was unlike anything the three kingdoms had ever seen. There was a marriage and alliance between Lemeth and Tardyn, and the lost twin royals of Ardia had returned. As the musicians struck up a jig everyone began dancing—everyone, that is, except Emberlynn and Aaver. They saw each other from across the room and ran to each other. Aaver picked her up, spinning her around and placing her gently on the floor. Then he took her in his arms and kissed her. Both Damian and Aedyn stood stunned when they saw this.

"Did you know about this?" Damian asked his cousin.

"Absolutely not. Don't you think I would have intervened if I'd known my best friend was cavorting with my sister?" he asked, laughing.

Emberlynn and Aaver stopped kissing, realizing everyone was staring. They had heard the exchange between Damian and Aedyn and they stood there, now, smiling guiltily back at them.

"We all have our secrets," she said, sheepishly.

She and Aaver burst out laughing.

EPILOGUE

It was a mild evening in late August and the sun was setting over the palace at Gillodel. If you walked inside you would find it empty—everyone was gathered at the Eastern edge of the garden. The sky fire seemed to dance that night, and silver rain fell from the sky as if Snow White's stars were stooping to kiss the bride. This, of course, was Audrianna's special touch.

Emberlynn had chosen not to wear a traditional cumbersome gown. Instead she walked down the aisle of rose pedals barefoot in a flowing white dress that she'd made herself. It had cap sleeves and diamond detailing. Her tiara rested on a mountain of golden curls, and she was even wearing her great grandmother's fairy necklace; Aaver was able to charm it so the fairy dust didn't affect her.

The groom wore a simple white tunic with green trousers. A small silver star on a chain was around his neck—a simple, but precious gift from his beautiful bride. On this perfect starlit night, Aaver, son of the recently reinstated Duke of Kingston, became prince of Ardia.

The couple planned to spend two weeks in Tardyn before returning to Eiladuén. It was the one place the princess had always wanted to go, and she couldn't wait to see the cliffs of Gelmyrh. Sierra had taken care of all the accommodations for her new cousin.

When the ceremony was over, they adjourned to the great hall for dancing and feasting. Audrianna met her brother and sister-in-law on the palace steps. She carried a large pack on her shoulder.

"I wanted to say goodbye before I left," she said.

"So you're really going, then?" Emberlynn asked.

"I can't stay here," she replied, as Damian and Sierra walked past.

"You're always welcome to stay with us in Ardia," Aaver offered.

"I know," she said, "But I need to get away for a while; clear my head and figure things out."

"Where will you go?"

"West."

"All that lies west of here are the Banwen Mountains and the Enalei Desert," said Emberlynn.

"And whatever lies beyond that." Audrianna added.

"But doesn't that scare you?"

She shrugged.

"We spent three years in the west after our exile, with one of the desert tribes."

"So that's where my husband learned his fencing skills."

Aaver grinned.

"I'm really gonna miss you, sis," he said, kissing her on the cheek.

"Me too," echoed Emberlynn, pulling her new sister in for a hug.

"I promise I'll visit as soon as I return."

"Good. And when you 'figure things out,' remember I've got a brother who's still a bachelor," Emberlynn said with a wink. "And he's crown prince of Ardia."

Audrianna laughed.

"I'll keep that in mind," she said.

With that, she turned and headed toward the stables. A few minutes later she rode out, and the couple stood watching until they saw her horse disappear into the darkness. Then Aaver turned to his bride.

"Shall we?" he asked, offering her his arm.

She took it, leaning in for a quick kiss. Then they walked up the steps, into the palace, and to the great hall where their friends and family were waiting.